BLOOD SONG

BLOOD SONG

THE FIRST BOOK OF LHARMELL

Rhiannon Hart

RANDOM HOUSE AUSTRALIA

A Random House book
Published by Random House Australia Pty Ltd
Level 3, 100 Pacific Highway, North Sydney NSW 2060
www.randomhouse.com.au

First published by Random House Australia in 2011

Addresses for companies within the Random House Group can be found at
www.randomhouse.com.au/offices.

National Library of Australia
Cataloguing-in-Publication Entry

Author: Hart, Rhiannon
Title: Blood Song / Rhiannon Hart
ISBN: 978 1 74275 096 5 (pbk.)
Series: Hart, Rhiannon. Lharmell; bk. 1
Target audience: For young adults
Dewey number: A823.4

Main cover image by Megan Kennedy, featuring original photograph by
Ana Gremard. Eagle photograph ©istockphoto.com/JamesBrey
Cat photograph ©dreamstime.com/Kipuxa
Cover design by DesignCherry
Internal design by Midland Typesetters, Australia
Typeset in Garamond 12.5/17pt by Midland Typesetters, Australia
Printed in Australia by Griffin Press, an acredited ISO AS/NZS
14001:2004 Environmental Management System printer

10 9 8 7 6 5 4 3 2 1

The paper this book is printed on is certified against
the Forest Stewardship Council® Standards. Griffin
Press holds FSC chain of custody certification SGS-
COC-005088. FSC promotes environmentally
responsible, socially beneficial and economically viable
management of the world's forests.

FSC
www.fsc.org
MIX
Paper from
responsible sources
FSC® C009448

For my mum and dad

ONE

I was thinking of blood again so I went to practise my archery. That's what I always did when I thought I was going to kill something. I hit the bullseye every time and nothing had died yet, so at least I had that going for me.

I didn't know any other sixteen-year-old girls but the ones in my books didn't obsessively fire arrows because they felt the urge to bite someone. They worried about suitors and ribbons and things. Then again, a few got fed to dragons, so I seemed to have it better than some.

There was still an hour before sundown but the forest around me was blackening into an early twilight. The light barely mattered; I could practise well into the night if I wanted to, still firing perfect shots.

Leap was curled up on my discarded cloak. His eyes were slitted and he watched me, purring when I glanced at him. Far above us Griffin was hovering over the clearing, golden wings spread against a steely sky.

My feet were tangled in the long, unkempt grass. The grounds of the Amentine palace were once the most magnificent in all southern Brivora. Now, they have fallen into disrepair. As the wealth of the House of Amentia trickled away over many generations, so too did the magnificence of the palace. The gardens were weedy and overgrown. The forest had reclaimed the land, and uncut saplings had become towering oaks. Ivy had crept inexorably up the steep castle walls, reaching far above my head to touch the windowsill of my lofty bedroom.

By the time my mother took the crown as queen, the disorder was complete. It would take huge sums of money to repair not only the gardens to their former magnificence, but also the crumbling castle, the spreading mould and unfashionable décor – money we didn't have. It was easier for my mother simply to shut up the unusable parts of the keep. So this was what she did.

I preferred it in the grounds where there were still tracts of scraggy grass and I could set up my archery range, the forest enveloping me on four sides.

The world had all but forgotten our existence, but I found I did not mind so much. I liked my solitude. If given the choice, I would prefer to stay that way forever.

But we wouldn't. Lilith was to be married. And sometime soon, all too soon, it would be my turn for a husband. As Second Daughter I would have to make my home with my husband in his kingdom, wherever that should be.

I grimaced, and swiped another arrow from my quiver. My skin crawled at the thought of someone touching me.

Lilith, on the other hand, had always detested our home for its chilly and ramshackle nature, and was looking forward to her marriage to Prince Lester and life as the future Queen of Varlint. Amentia was hers by inheritance but I doubted she would rule it from its rightful seat. Rather she would reign by proxy from Varlint. Perhaps Amentia had seen its last queen.

I notched the arrow, which I had fletched myself with Griffin's golden feathers, and aimed at the target thirty feet away. I drew back on the taut string, my eyes narrowing, seeing nothing but the ringed red circle.

Before I could fire I was distracted by the urgent drumming of hoof beats approaching rapidly. I tried to shut out the noise but the horse's scream as it was pulled to a sudden halt made me start.

'Drat.' I lowered my bow and waited, ears cocked towards the keep.

Silence.

I raised my bow and drew back on the string. I had the red dot in my sights again when voices reached my ears. I couldn't make out the words but the speakers were agitated. Again I lowered my bow, preferring to wait until the interruption ceased. I glanced at Leap; he was tucked into a tight ball, his short silvery fur fluffed out against the cold. His purr rumbled deep in his chest, and he flexed his claws luxuriously.

I was raising my bow for the third time when a cry rang out. It was sharp and defiant, the noise evaporating quickly in the brittle air.

Lilith.

'Oh, blast it all!' I cried, hurling my bow to the ground, where it bounced harmlessly in the long grass. My concentration was ruined so I bent to unstring the bow. There was no point practising any more today. I would have words with my sister when I got inside. She had no respect for –

I noticed that Leap had lifted his head and his ears were pricked in the direction of the castle. His pupils dilated and he raised himself into a crouch.

My breath caught. Something was wrong.

I shoved my arrows back in the quiver, shame burning my cheeks. Any normal girl would have flown to her sister's aid without a second thought. I held my gauntleted wrist aloft and let out an ear-splitting whistle, calling down my eagle. She drew in her wings and dropped like a stone, only at the very last second flapping them to alight on my arm. Her black eyes flashed, and I saw that she too was craning towards the castle, unease visible in the set of her sleek wings.

I grabbed my cloak and together we raced to the western entrance, a damp and mouldering side door that was seldom used by anyone but me. The stairwell was near pitch-black, but I was guided upwards by the sound of my steps echoing off the stone floor. We emerged on a landing and Griffin flew from my arm, heading for my mother's sitting room. Leap followed, ears flat.

At the chamber door I was greeted by a tableau of despair. Lilith lay prostrate on the floor, her shoulders heaving with sobs. My mother, Renata, was crouched beside her, tenderly smoothing Lilith's red-gold hair from her brow. In her hand she clutched a parchment.

'What is it? What has happened?' I asked from

the doorway. The rawness of their emotions made me reluctant to approach. I always made a hash of my attempts to comfort others.

Renata held up the parchment. 'A messenger arrived with this from Varlint. Lester is dead,' she said.

'Lester!' He couldn't be dead. He was simply vibrant with life: bellowing, thumping and grinning at everything, and always in the rudest of health. I'd put up with his violent cheerfulness on many occasions since he'd become my sister's betrothed.

At our mother's words Lilith began to sob even harder.

'How?'

'A hunting accident,' my mother told me. There was grief on her face, but something else as well: fear. This wasn't just a blow to Lilith. It was bad news for the whole country.

Leap, who was a sensitive creature, padded over and butted his head against my sister's shoulder. She reacted brutally, shoving him and crying out, 'Get away, you filthy beast! Get away!'

Leap jumped onto a chair, his tail lashing with annoyance.

'Lilith!'

'Take it out, Zeraphina,' Renata snapped. 'Can't you see she's upset?'

Miffed, I scooped Leap up and made for the door. It, it, it. *He* has a *name*.

Lilith had never liked my animals. She found their cleverness creepy and complained they watched her with disapproving looks on their faces. Which was ridiculous. Griffin couldn't manage disapproving. She could only look fierce.

Renata gathered Lilith into her arms, rocking her gently. I should have stayed to comfort my sister but all I could feel once I'd left the room was relief.

Carrying Leap, I made for my bed chamber. A flash of gold overhead told me that Griffin would beat us there. A candle was burning at my bedside, but I blew it out. It was near full dark and I pulled the tapestry curtains back from my window and gazed out. In the northern sky the clouds had broken up in places and a sliver of moon was visible. I felt a strange tug on my insides as I looked in that direction. Leap purred in my arms, the reflection of the bats flying to their feeding grounds dancing in his eyes.

I wondered how Lester had died. Whether his belly had been wrenched open by a boar's tusk, or if he'd been thrown from a horse to meet a hasty end by way of a broken neck.

Was there blood? I wondered.

The days that followed were unbearable. The grief within our castle walls was palpable and it completely threw my aim off.

Our mother wept for Lester as hard as Lilith, but her reasons were rather more mercenary.

'I won't marry anyone now,' Lilith swore tearfully in the days after Lester's death. 'I don't want anyone but Lester.'

Renata, in her typical fashion, ignored the wishes of her eldest daughter. She sent a flurry of letters to every royal seat with an unmarried prince, telling them of her 'fortuitously available daughter'.

I'm sure Lester's parents wouldn't have put it quite that way.

From my bedroom window high up in the keep, I watched the suitors arrive, and even from that height I could see what a sorry bunch they were: paunches, bald spots, and limp white hands abounded. One sat on his horse with his legs sticking straight out in the stirrups and bounced along like a rubber ball.

Lilith refused the lot of them, sight unseen, from her bedchamber.

Then one day, a letter arrived from Pergamia, the most powerful kingdom in all Brivora. My mother's lady-in-waiting put the letter with its golden seal into Renata's hands as Lilith and I looked on, dumbstruck.

'It's not . . . it surely can't be . . . is it?' Lilith said, her black satin handkerchief for once forgotten in her hand.

Renata broke the seal and read quickly.

'It is an offer of marriage,' she said, not bothering to hide the astonishment in her voice. 'Pending a meeting between you and Prince Amis, the king's only son.' She gripped her daughter's arm. 'Darling, we are saved! Don't you see? Amis will be king one day. And you – you shall be queen.'

For a second, Lilith's eyes shone at the prospect: she, the princess of an obscure, downtrodden queendom, wedded to the richest, most powerful prince in all the land, and destined to be queen. Then she remembered Lester, and her eyes dimmed. She dabbed at her dry eyes with the handkerchief. 'Mother, I am in mourning.'

Renata's green eyes darkened to storm cloud proportions. I removed to a safe distance.

From that moment, our lives became a living hell. Renata screamed at Lilith. Lilith screamed at Renata. Griffin screamed at nothing at all and Leap looked permanently haunted. I could find no peace even in the furthest reaches of the forest.

Meal times were the worst, vitriol turning the food in our mouths to ashes.

One evening Renata ceased trying to reason with Lilith and simply commanded, 'Daughter, you will go, you will marry him, and you will like it!'

Lilith put down her knife and fork, her jaw set. 'No, Mother. I refuse. You can go on until you are blue in the face but I *will not marry that man*. Lester –' Saying his name made her tearful, and she paused to take a breath. 'Lester has been gone less than a month and already you want to replace him with some stranger from the north.'

The north? I looked up from the broccoli I'd been pushing around my plate. Of course, Pergamia was in the north. But why did that thought give me pause?

A memory unfurled in my mind. Or rather, a sense of déjà vu as I was certain the vision that came to me wasn't anything I had seen with my earthly eyes. I glimpsed great black trees swathed in mist and heard the surge of water as if the sea was lapping at my heels. Lights danced among the trees, in pairs like glowing eyes.

The temperature of the room seemed to plummet as if I really did stand in that bleak landscape. Keening filled the air, and craggy mountains rose against a sky encrusted with stars. I felt a tug in my chest as if something was pulling me forward, and curiosity turned to horror as I felt the onset of the blood-hunger, the monstrous cravings I kept secret that tormented my days and nights and would flare up without warning. They began with breathlessness and cramping, and usually ended up with me writhing on the floor in agony.

'Dead, darling, dead,' Renata was muttering. 'Once you say it you might start to get over it.'

Her voice came from far away, as if through water. I clenched my hands on my dress, terrified they would notice the pain etched on my face. It took all my effort not to cry out.

'I don't know how long we can keep up this charade,' Renata continued. Her full attention was on Lilith, and she evidently didn't notice that her younger daughter was dying at the other end of the table. 'The coffers are emptying, and if I don't do something quickly people will begin to know. I either find a way to prevent the frosts that are killing the crops, or one of you has to marry very well. As you're the eldest, and Zeraphina is only sixteen and still a year away from marriageable age, it's up to you to get us out of this.'

The burning subsided slightly and I could breathe again. I blinked and looked around. No one had noticed.

Lilith was exasperated. 'Out of what? Being poor? What is so bad about that?'

'Nothing, dear,' Renata replied with exaggerated patience. 'But once word gets out that we can't raise a proper army, what do you think will happen to us?'

I hadn't thought of that. Judging by the look on Lilith's face, neither had she.

'So I'm to marry for money,' she wailed. 'I was going to marry for love. Oh, Lester! How could you be so careless?' She dissolved into sobs, pushing her plate away and cradling her head in her hands.

'Yes, yes, hysterics will solve everything. In case you've forgotten, I'm the one who chose Lester in the first place, and for exactly the same reason you're to marry Amis Pergamon: he's rich.'

'But Lester loved me. Why would this man want to marry a pauper?'

Renata took a deep breath. 'As I said, no one knows the state of our affairs –'

'So I'm to deceive him?'

'Daughter, no one's deceiving anyone if he falls in love with you.'

'But what about me? What if I don't love him?'

'Darling, I rather think I don't care.'

Lilith let out another wail and fled to her room.

'I didn't say you could leave the table!'

I could see Griffin shuffling impatiently by the door. She wanted to hunt, and I wanted to get away. There was a residual tightness in my chest that might flare up at any second. 'May I go?'

Renata sighed. 'Go, go.'

I jumped up and headed for the door, but she called, 'Zeraphina, do you think me a monster?'

'No, Mother.' I put my left foot over my right, trying not to shuffle about.

'I just want her to do her duty. I've always treated her well, haven't I?'

What was appropriate here? A hug? Gushing assurance? I wasn't sure I could manage the proper sincerity at that moment so I settled for a nod.

'How did this happen?' she said softly. 'Amentia was struggling when I became queen, but things were never this bad. Winter has eclipsed all other seasons.' She sighed. 'At times like this I wish your father was still alive.'

I was surprised, as I rarely heard her speak of him.

'He would have no qualms about beating her into it.'

Oh.

Renata smiled weakly. 'Off you go.'

I paced dreamily down the corridor to my room.

My senses tingled. I breathed deeply, smelling the damp stone of the castle, the snow on the wind. I fancied I could hear small creatures crawling among the leaf litter in the forest.

We reached my bedroom and Griffin flew from my wrist, out the open window and into the night. Leap sat with me on the windowsill and we gazed towards the north. The horizon was darkest there and where the clouds parted I could see a sky scattered heavily with stars. I felt the tug again. That place I had seen, the land of keening voices and great black trees, it lay in that direction. And it was calling to me.

———

I lay awake most of the night, feeling the pull of the north like a compass needle to a magnet. What did it mean that I felt the blood-hunger just seconds after I saw the vision of that strange land? The hunger frightened me, and I was ashamed of it. I feared what would happen to me if someone found out about it. It wasn't normal to crave blood. It was monstrous, but monsters were no more than made-up creatures in tales to scare little children, or the delusions of a mad person. Did that make me mad?

The compulsion to go north nagged at me through the night. I argued with myself, back and forth, reasoning that I might discover what was wrong with me if I went northward, and then that it was foolish to even comtemplate such a thing. It could be terribly dangerous. There was something not right about that black forest.

Sometime before dawn, restlessness forced my decision. It was foolish to remain at home if Lilith travelled northwards to meet Prince Amis. Cowering at home would accomplish nothing.

If she would go.

The hunger thrummed through me. She must go.

When the keep began to stir, I wrapped a wool shawl around my nightgown and, taking my tea tray with me, I paced the freezing flagstones to Lilith's room.

She was curled on her bedroom chair and wrapped in a blanket, her tea tray lying untouched beside her. I poured her a cup, added lemon and sugar and handed it to her. She accepted it automatically, still gazing out the window at the freezing morning. From this high up we could see the tree-tops of the surrounding forest and a lot of heavy grey cloud. Far off, the Teripsiin Mountains rose steeply, their caps permanently frozen white and disappearing into the overcast sky.

'Thinking about Lester?' I asked.

She nodded.

I sat down on the rug at her feet, curling the fur from her bed around me. Despite the fires burning in the grates, the tapestries on the walls and the thick rugs on the floor, our rooms were always chilly.

From the doorway I saw Leap approaching, his eyes on my lap and a purr starting up. He liked to be cuddled on cold mornings but I surreptitiously shooed him away, not wanting to provoke Lilith. He stopped, his eyes widening. Then he gave a quick lash of his tail and stalked off.

'Sister,' I began. 'I must confess that I never liked Lester. He lacked northern manners, don't you agree?'

Lilith glared down at me. 'What would you know about northern manners? You've never been to the north.'

'Well, neither have you,' I pointed out. 'Shouldn't you see it before you become an old married woman? Even if you decide not to marry Prince Amis, you should at least travel a little.'

Lilith turned her pale face back to the window. 'Zeraphina, why in the world do you even care?' Her voice was incredibly tired.

That stung. I cared about things.

I cared about the north.

I squashed that thought and tried another tack. 'Lester wouldn't want you sitting around pining yourself to death, would he?'

Lilith shrugged. The dull morning light made her look colourless, and her wan features told me that she hadn't slept well the night before, or any night since Lester had died.

'A change of scenery might help, mightn't it? It could be like a holiday. We could go to the north and –' I shrugged – 'just look around.' I winced. I was making it sound as inconsequential as a picnic.

'I want to forget him,' Lilith whispered. 'I just want everything to stop. I try to look ahead and it's like there's nothing there.' Her eyes were bleak.

'There's the north,' I offered.

'Do shut up about the north. You're as bad as Mother.'

We fell silent. I was out of ideas so I poured myself some tea and clutched the cup between my hands, the warmth spreading through my fingers.

Outside, the sky was heavy with snow. Soon a powdery white layer would blanket the land and

Amentia would grow even colder and bleaker. Another harvest season had come to an end and the granaries were near-empty. The people were living on the stores that were meant for next season's planting. Mother would have her work cut out assuring them that first Lester's kingdom and now Amis's would bail us out.

I would turn seventeen next autumn – nearly a year away, but not long enough as far as I was concerned. For all I knew, Renata had already sent the letters out. Advertising her daughter. I shivered, and not from the cold. I dreaded another's hands on me. They would find out what I was. They would be able to feel it through my skin, the monster that tormented me, that had dark hungers and urges I didn't understand. Or the hunger would give me away, the fits that left me gasping and writhing on the floor. Fortunately they remained unwitnessed, but it was only a matter of time.

But what if rather than marrying some prince, I had another destiny, one that lay to the north? I had to find out why I was being called there.

'I hear it's warm in the north,' I said. 'You could escape the winter. Go swimming. Pick berries.'

Lilith was silent, but I could see her thinking about it. She hated winter in Amentia.

'Wouldn't that be nicer than being cooped up in this gloomy old castle for three or four months? It's going to be a hard winter, you know. Don't you feel you'll just go mad here?'

Lilith groaned. 'Oh, all right! I'll go, I'll go.'

I gave a yip of delight and clutched her arm.

'Watch the tea! Why are you so excited?'

My whole body was zinging. *The north!* I knew it was unreasonable to be reacting this way and I tried to rein in my enthusiasm. 'Well, I'm going with you, of course. I'm sick of the cold, too.'

Lilith gave me a questioning look, but didn't say anything.

I should have been ashamed of my lies, but all I felt was the most intense exhilaration. We were going to the north.

———

Mother was ecstatic when we told her the news. She was poring over the latest figures from the treasury when I yanked Lilith into her chamber.

'We're going!' I cried.

She was ecstatic, I was ecstatic, but the bride-to-be looked positively miserable.

'I'm not even out of mourning,' she complained. 'It's unseemly.'

'Mourning is for peasants,' Renata proclaimed, and called in her lady-in-waiting. 'Eugenia, summon the tailor, the dressmaker – Wakefield, not that second-rate one – milliner, corsetière, shoemaker, coach-maker, perfumier, and cosmetician. And the hairdresser.' The woman bobbed and went to leave. 'And take those dreadful papers away,' Renata called, pointing to the accounts. 'Tell the treasurer I'm not to be bothered with them any more.'

'Mother!' Lilith was aghast. 'Won't all that be terribly expensive?'

'Do you think we're going to turn up at the House of Pergamon dressed in sackcloth and ashes with our begging bowls out?'

Soon the nine most prestigious couturiers in the queendom were gathered in Renata's quarters. She lined them up and lectured them like they were about to go into battle. 'We're going to need travelling clothes. The people must see our procession through the cities, and it's got to look good. We need to raise morale. Then we'll need more clothes for when we reach Pergamia; lighter, more summery ones, and these ones have to look very good. Then we're going to need more for our stay at the palace, and these ones have to look *stunning*. Plus there's the trousseau for Lilith.'

'I'm not even betrothed yet,' Lilith protested.

'As good as, darling. Do you want a Pergamian tailor designing your wedding dress? No, we'll get it made here.'

'Don't you think it's a little presumptuous that I show up at this stranger's palace with my wedding clothes?'

'No, it's expected. I know best, Lilith.'

I felt myself grow anxious. How long was this all going to take? I had thought we would just pack up and leave.

Renata turned back to the assembled craftspeople. 'Now, this is the most important part: this isn't Varlint we're going to, it Pergamia. We need to look rich. We need to look so rich that we're not even aware of how many pots of gold we have lying around. Those mousey clothes that Lilith wore for her last betrothal just won't do.' She clapped her hands. 'Now go! I want to see styles and fabric samples this afternoon.' Renata sighed happily and turned back to us. 'This is going to be fun.'

TWO

It was a living hell.

Renata was belting the tailor over the head with his own designs. 'Rubbish! Rot! Pigswill!' she cried, punctuating each of her words with a fresh thwack.

The milliner and the corsetière stood in the corner, knowing it was their turn next.

Lilith and I were sitting on a couch in Renata's sitting room, surrounded by fabric samples, ribbons, buttons, beadwork and sketches. It was the third day of preparation and we were both beginning to think that wintering in the palace wouldn't be so bad after all.

'We may as *well* turn up in sackcloth and ashes rather than these designs. But perhaps even that would be beyond your skill? Now go away and come back when you can produce something that doesn't make me want to boil you in oil.'

The tailor tried to retrieve his designs from Renata, but she brandished them again and he scuttled off.

'Next!' Renata said, throwing the drawings onto the fire.

'She's in her element, isn't she?' Lilith whispered to me.

I nodded. 'I've never seen her like this. Not even when we went to Varlint.'

'Do you think she really needs us?'

'If we ask to leave, what are the chances she'll throw *us* on the fire?' I asked. 'But then again, I don't see why I have to be here –'

Lilith gripped my arm. 'If you leave me with her I'll make my new husband find you a saggy old duke to marry. One with warts,' she hissed.

Renata came over with a scrap of lace from the corsetière. 'How about this for your wedding night, Lilith?'

Lilith snatched it away, going red. 'Mother!' She dropped her voice to a whisper, glancing at the milliner. 'There are men in the room.'

'Don't be so precious, darling. Everyone in court is going to see you tucked up in bed in this nightgown.'

Lilith stopped going red and turned white. 'What?'

'Oh, didn't you know? They practically turn the wedding night into a carnival in Pergamia,' Renata said, holding the fabric up to the light. 'And then there's the morning after.'

'What happens the morning after?' I asked.

'They display the bedsheet.'

Lilith looked horrified. She was so shy of her body that even I hadn't seen her in less than her nightgown since she was eight. 'Why do they display the bedsheet?'

'So that everyone knows that the bride was pure, and that any child that turns up nine months later almost definitely belongs to the husband.'

'*Almost* definitely?'

'Yes, darling. Brides have been known to have indiscretions after the sheet is taken down.'

'I would never!'

'Yes, yes, of course. You know, I always thought it would be rather odd, having breakfast in court under the conjugal evidence,' Renata mused. 'But that's just the way they do things in Pergamia.'

I began to snort with laughter. Lilith pinched my arm.

'Ow! What? It's funny,' I protested.

Amid the chaos of our preparations, I found myself needing – longing – to know more about the north. I couldn't wait any longer.

A few days later, while Renata and Lilith were occupied with wedding dresses, I snuck down to the library. I pushed the huge oak doors open and they groaned on their hinges. We didn't use the place much, not since Lilith and I had finished our schooling. It contained lots of stuffy books, the sort you read only if you're made to.

It was dark, but I hadn't brought a candle with me. I knew I wouldn't need it as my eyesight was excellent. I sniffed and smelt mildew and mice, a wholly disgusting odour. Leap smelt it too, and got wide-eyed and disappeared among the stacks. Almost immediately a petrified squeaking started up.

I walked around in the gloom, trying to remember where the geography books were kept. There was mathematics, and science . . . I spied them on a high shelf and wheeled the ladder over. Perched on the fifth rung I ran my fingers over the spines: *History of the World* and *Atlas of the World*, just what I needed. The atlas was a huge book, more than half the length of my body, and after I pulled it from the shelf I had to drop it to the ground. It landed with a *whump* that sent clouds of dust into the air. I climbed down after it with the history book and took them both to a table.

I opened the atlas first. On the inside cover was a huge map of the world, marked out by a grid. I quickly found Amentia, a pitifully small country on the continent of Brivora. Tracing my finger northwards I found Pergamia, a large nation that covered all of northern Brivora. North of Pergamia a white hole stared out at me, as if the cartographer had gone for a cup of tea and forgotten to finish the map. I frowned. That was odd. Was it uncharted territory, or a section that had been left deliberately blank? If the latter, the purpose of such a thing evaded me.

I turned to the history book. I eyed its title carefully, but it did indeed read *History of the World*. I would have been happier if the subtitle read *Yes, that's the WHOLE world*, but it would have to do.

I scanned the index for an entry labelled 'uncharted territory', but there wasn't one. The book didn't have a map so it was impossible to compare it to the atlas. Not knowing what else to do, I looked up Pergamia. There was quite a long, boring passage about past kings and queens, commerce, population, agriculture and so on, but then a paragraph caught my eye:

Pergamia has long been at war with Lharmell. Little is known about the country other than that it lies to the north of the Straits of Unctium.

To the north! I read on excitedly.

Pergamia has never shared any knowledge of Lharmell or the Lharmellins with the rest of the world, and even many Pergamians know little of their northern neighbours.

There was no other mention of Lharmell on that page. I flicked to the index and looked it up, but there was no entry for it other than the one I had read. That was it? Two measly sentences about a whole country?

An investigation of the other history books failed to turn up any other mention of Lharmell. In frustration I hurled a pile of books to the floor and stalked out. Covered in cobwebs and with a mouse dangling limply from his jaws, Leap followed.

As I neared my bedroom I could hear Renata calling me. Her voice had taken on a shrill note and I realised she must have been calling for some time. She would want to talk about dresses or some such. Well, I wasn't in the mood. I went to my room and slammed the door.

She stormed in after me. 'Where have you been? The dressmaker is here for a fitting.'

I threw myself down on my bed. 'I don't feel like it.'

Renata put her hands on her hips. 'Don't be difficult, Zeraphina. No one's making you go on this trip.'

I jumped up again. She had a point.

In her room, I tried on dress after dress.

'Dark blue, mauve and black go best with her colouring,' Renata told the dressmaker as she watched the proceedings with folded arms. 'Cream as well, but we'll save the light colours for Lilith. I'm not going to have another awkward time in Pergamia like we did in Varlint. We're going to emphasise Zeraphina's difference, have it all out in the open so people don't gossip.'

My *difference*. She meant the way I looked. I was so starkly different from my mother and sister that people were wont to whisper about my parentage, which mortified me and whipped my mother into seething rages. She and Lilith had auburn hair and green eyes, as once had I. But as a child I caught a rare disease. It had almost killed me, and placed such stresses on my tiny body that it had leached the colour from my eyes until they resembled a lake under a thick layer of ice, and turned my hair only a few shades from the deepest black.

I stood, arms outstretched, in a gown made from yards and yards of wine-coloured satin while the dressmaker fiddled with the sleeves. They were fitted, and the gown was tight to the hips and flared out into a full skirt. My bust, what little there was of it, was being pushed violently upwards by a corset.

'Perfect,' Renata announced. 'Now the Pergamian gowns.'

I breathed a sigh of relief when the corset came off. It would be too hot for such things in Pergamia. I was dressed in delicate sleeveless silk dresses and sandals with straps that coiled up my calves. I practised walking in the sweeping gowns, instructed by Renata how to show just the right amount of ankle.

'She looks quite fetching. You know, Daughter, the winter court in Pergamia is going to be filled with single young princes. We can get a head-start on your betrothal. You're not to go looking at the barons, though. A lady must always marry above her station.'

The pleasure I got from the pretty dresses dried up. I didn't want to look fetching, not to barons and not to anyone else. 'I'm only sixteen, Mother, remember?'

'It's never too early to start looking,' Renata murmured as she twitched a fold of fabric into place. She looked up at the dressmaker. 'Good. Have these ready by tomorrow. We leave in two days.'

Two days. I clutched my thumbs in my fists in anticipation.

———

I was gazing out my bedroom window at the north. The wind was blowing. I couldn't move, but I could hear a keening on the wind, like a thousand voices raised in a strange chant. Harmonies eddied on the breeze like water in a stream. The notes rose and fell and tumbled over one another with exquisite unpredictability. I was mesmerised, and felt a little feverish.

Behind me my luggage was stacked in a huge pile. We were leaving for Pergamia in the morning.

But there was something else in my room. Something moving about. Awareness prickled down my spine. A faint, white-blue glow fell on the windowsill, the light coming from whatever was behind me. I wanted to turn but I was held captive by the song on the wind. Such beautiful music. So hypnotic. I yearned for the singers, to be with them, to join in their song. The thread anchored in my chest tugged hard.

The voices grew louder, and as the song began its crescendo I felt my heart contract with longing.

I'm coming, I told the voices. *Please, wait for me.* I felt tears of despair prick my eyes. They were so very far away.

Behind me, the thing spoke, its voice faint but insistent over the strange music.

Zeraphina . . .

I started. It knew my name. I heard it not with my ears but from deep inside myself, as if it was speaking the word for my soul.

It was becoming difficult to breathe, each gasp now more painful than the last. I felt like I was being wrenched in two by my fear and desire.

The thing behind me was hovering close. My hands, resting on the windowsill, were bathed in its cold blue light. The being radiated chill, but as I was burning up the coolness was a balm. Then whatever it was touched me everywhere at once and I stopped thinking altogether.

I was enveloped in a tender embrace. Sweet coolness spread like running water through my body, dousing the burning hunger. The wind dropped, and with it the strange singing died away. I found I could move again.

I turned, and pale eyes stared into mine, dazzling me with their brilliance. In them was echoed my own feelings of intense longing. No one had ever looked at me that way before. So tender and yet so hungry.

I smiled into the blue eyes, enraptured by their glow.

Yes? I said to it in my mind, unable to speak but sure it could hear me. *You called my name?*

It didn't respond, but stayed where it was, floating in front of me. The pleasant, shivery feeling made me bold. I reached out to touch it and *snap!* It disappeared like a candle being snuffed out. The sudden release made me stagger.

I looked about. I *was* standing in front of the window, and the cold, silent wind was whipping at my nightgown.

I heard growling, and searched the shadows for my cat. He was under the bed, rigid with fear. I dragged him out and held him, but he sat awkwardly in my arms, paws pressed against me as he stared wide-eyed around the room.

'You saw it too?' I muttered. I was suddenly frightened of the shadows. Like a child, I jumped into bed and pulled the covers over my head. Leap curled against my churning stomach. I shook with cold and fear, hoping it had all been a bad dream.

Sleep was beyond me. I lay awake, my mind racing, until the first light of dawn touched my windowsill. Then, made brave by the grey morning sun, I got up. I was already bathed and wrapped in a towel when Renata and her lady-in-waiting swept in. I didn't have my own maid, something I was thankful for as it would have been ridiculous for me to get dressed up every day just to shoot my bow and arrow by myself. But Renata was adamant that on this trip we were all to be groomed within an inch of our lives every step of the way.

'Eugenia is here to dress you and do your hair. Don't dawdle,' Renata said – quite unnecessarily I felt as I had already got myself up – before hurrying back to Lilith.

My travelling clothes for the first day of our journey had been laid out the night before. I had a mauve satin gown with a pearl-like lustre, cut in the Amentine style. Over it I would wear a black velvet hooded cloak lined with mauve silk.

I was putting on my jewellery while Eugenia did up the many little buttons at my back, when I noticed a piece was missing. I had two silver rings that I liked to wear on my thumbs, but one of them was gone. I couldn't see it on the floor, and I was down on my knees scrabbling under the bed when Eugenia cried, 'Your gown! Miss Zeraphina, your mother will go spare if you dirty it.'

It wasn't under the bed. I stood quietly while Eugenia finished my toilet, but my mind was in turmoil. So it hadn't been a bad dream. Both rings had been there the night before. I distinctly remembered having taken them off at bedtime and putting them in my jewellery box. Someone – or something – had stolen it in the night. The phantom? The thing had seemed intangible, a mere spirit as it had hovered before me. But perhaps it had form enough to steal things. I wondered what it might want with my ring. Conduct voodoo? Black magic? I thought it had spoken tenderly, but in hindsight I wondered if there had been a hint of menace in its tone.

Eugenia finished my hair, bobbed, and left me gazing out the window, twisting the single silver ring on my thumb.

Perhaps this was a mistake, and I shouldn't be going to Pergamia after all. I had no idea what was waiting for me in the north. Maybe it was malevolent. Maybe it wanted me for evil purposes and I should be resisting, not acquiescing.

As I imagined not getting into the carriage that

waited downstairs and instead waving goodbye to Renata and Lilith as they set out for the north, pain flooded my body and my stomach cramped violently. It felt like my bones were being torn out of my body. Bent double, I gasped for air.

I'll go! I screamed in my head. *I'll get in the coach, I promise. Please stop*, I begged. After a minute the pain subsided, as if whatever it was had been satisfied. The phantom? The singers? I slowly stood up straight. It seemed that not going north was a physical impossibility. I cursed the thing that had stolen my ring. It must have known I would have second thoughts at the last minute and had taken it for some evil, manipulating purpose.

Lilith was at my door. 'Ready?' She looked pale and scared, but for the first time in weeks, she looked hopeful. And beautiful. Her long hair had been set in waves that cascaded down her back. She wore a pure white cloak edged with white fox fur, and in her hair was a silver circlet that signified she was the First Daughter of the House of Amentia.

'Just about. I'll meet you downstairs.' I needed to take a few deep breaths and compose myself.

The coachmen came in and started carting my boxes downstairs. There were an awful lot of them. It was astounding the number of dresses, cloaks, hats and pairs of shoes Renata thought I would need. And I wasn't even the one getting married.

I fastened on my gauntlet and whistled to Griffin. She came hurtling in through the window, her beak bloodied. A swift pang went through me at the sight, and I tried not to let the delicious scent of her fresh kill reach my nostrils.

Our coach stood on the flagstones, looking like an ornamented, oversized white pumpkin that had been hollowed out and upholstered with red velvet. Six white horses with red plumes were hitched to it and they pranced impatiently on the frosty ground, snorting vapour from their nostrils. In front were two horsemen holding the Amentine banner. Against a red background was a griffin, its lion claws bared and fire curling from its beak. It was the namesake for my own Griffin, both golden and triumphant.

Bringing up the rear of our convoy was the servant's coach, and more horsemen carrying pikes. As far as royal processions went, it was tiny.

As soon as Lilith saw me with Leap and Griffin she looked livid. 'You are not bringing those filthy creatures into the carriage.'

Renata was already seated inside and she leaned out the window, impatient to get going. 'Now what is it?'

'Mother, Zeraphina wants to bring her pets with her. Tell her they're disgusting and they're not getting into the carriage.'

'She's quite right, Zeraphina,' Renata said. 'You'll have to leave them here.'

My mouth fell open. 'Leave them here? I can't leave them here. Who would look after them?'

'No one needs to look after them. They're wild animals.' Lilith said this as if I was quite thick.

'Sister, I don't *take* them anywhere. They follow me. If I get in that coach they're going to want to get in after me. I can't help it.'

Lilith folded her arms. 'Then I'm not getting in.'

'Zeraphina.' Renata's voice held a warning note.

'Wait. Give me a moment.' I looked around for a place to put them. I picked Leap up and took him to the servants' coach. 'Excuse me,' I said through the window. 'Could you please take my cat? He's very friendly.' I handed a puzzled Leap through the window and prayed he would behave. Then I strode back to our carriage and put Griffin on some curly ornamentation next to the driver. She could hunt as she needed and keep an eye on things, as she liked to do. I wasn't worried she'd get lost. She and Leap seemed to be able to home in on me as if I were a beacon.

'There. Doesn't she look regal?' I smirked at Lilith and got into the coach.

Grudgingly, she got in behind me.

We were on our way to the north.

THREE

I'd forgotten how deadly dull and uncomfortable travelling by coach could be. After only three days sheer boredom had sunk in so deeply that we could do nothing but stare out the window at the barren, mountainous landscape. Books and small games lay forgotten in our laps. Snow had begun to fall, and while it was pretty it turned everything a uniform colour. This made the landscape even less interesting to look at, as snow here looked the same as snow there.

Every so often we would pass through a village or city and have to plaster fake smiles on our faces and wave endlessly at the townspeople. All throughout Amentia, everyone looked overworked, underfed, and desperate. I watched

Lilith's face as we travelled through the worst parts and she would bite her lip in consternation. If Renata hadn't convinced her that this arranged marriage was critical for the welfare of the people, then these sights would.

'How far is it to Pergamia now?' I asked Renata for the umpteenth time.

'Darling,' Renata said, not bothering to drag her gaze from the window. 'If yesterday we were fifteen days away from the capital, how many days away do you think we are now?'

'That means there's still another day before we even get out of Amentia. I'm freezing.' Lilith stamped her feet on the carriage floor.

We were all numb with cold from so much inactivity. Renata had her hands buried in an enormous fur muff and we all wore several layers, but still the cold seeped into our bones.

Some nights we stayed at an inn and could have a hot meal in front of a fire before sleeping in a warm bed. Other times we simply changed horses and continued on into the night, chewing bread and cheese and trying to sleep while we were jostled this way and that every time the carriage hit a pothole. Which was often. The roads in Amentia were in a bad state.

'My behind has gone to sleep,' I muttered, rubbing at it. I wanted to practise my archery and I was heartily sick of being dressed in so much finery in order to do nothing but sit in a coach all day.

Lilith shifted in her seat. 'Mother, tell us about Pergamia.'

Renata sighed but then slowly sat up. 'All right.'

I turned my attention to her, mildly interested. Pergamia was in the north, after all.

'Pergamia is a very large country,' she said, as if reciting words from a textbook. 'It's about the size of eleven Amentias. Many hundreds of thousands of people live there, mostly in the cities along the coast of the Straits of Unctium. The coast is spectacular, I'm told. White sandy beaches, crystal clear water. The capital, which is where we're going, is Xallentaria. It's filled with artisans and dressmakers, and as a nation they are very particular about aesthetics, which is why I took such care over our attire. They're very strict about protocol and rank, but throw some of the most wildly extravagant parties in all the land. Agriculture is their largest industry, but what they don't have are tin, copper and iron. That's where Amentia comes in, because the Teripsiin Mountains are full of metals. We just don't have the resources and equipment to mine them. Once Lilith has married Amis, we can forge a trade agreement between our two countries and get our economy moving again.'

'A trade agreement,' Lilith echoed, looking as if she didn't enjoy hearing her impending marriage put in purely economic terms.

'What about Lharmell?' I asked.

I had never seen my mother go white, but just then she turned the same colour as the snow outside. 'What *about* Lharmell?' she asked.

'I understand they're at war.'

'I see. And what else do you know about that place?'

I shrugged. 'Pretty much nothing.'

I caught a flash of relief in Renata's eyes, and my curiosity was piqued. There *was* something strange about Lharmell, and she knew what it was.

'Did you know that there's only one book in the library at home that refers to it?' I asked.

'Actually, I did know that.' Renata's eyes turned steely. 'Daughter, people do not talk about that place, especially in Pergamia. In light of where we're going I'd like you to remember that.' She turned and looked out the window.

'But –'

'No, Zeraphina, we are not discussing this. Please read your book.'

I fumed, angry at being blockaded. Why was everyone and everything so reluctant to tell me anything about Lharmell? If she knew that the library contained barely a mention of the place, then she must have been the one to see to its censorship. I couldn't imagine why she would do such a thing. If the blue-eyed phantom ever showed up again I would certainly fire a few questions at it about its homeland.

I glared at the window and my reflection glared back at me. Ice-blue eyes! The phantom's eyes were exactly like mine – not the same shape, but definitely the same unusual colour. Did it have the same sickness as me as a child? But that was silly, because what sort of sickness could a phantom catch? Unless it wasn't really a phantom. I had heard of powerful magicians who were said to send their souls long distances in a matter of moments. If we were the same, was I a magician too? But surely, such things were only stories.

I wanted to ask Renata about my sickness again, but I was sure she wouldn't tell me anything new. I was livid with frustration until it occurred to me that I'd never asked Lilith. I didn't want to talk of it in front of Renata as I knew she'd shut Lilith up, so I waited until night came and Renata started to snore.

The light from the moon was reflected off the snow and it was quite bright in the coach.

'Lilith,' I whispered. 'Are you awake?'

'Yes,' she said, her voice very tired.

'Do you remember how I got very sick as a baby?'

'Yes, you nearly died.'

'Do you remember what the sickness was called?'

Lilith frowned. 'No, I don't think so.'

'Can you try to remember? It might be important.'

'I don't know, why don't you ask Mother?'

'I want to hear it from you. Can't you remember anything at all?'

She opened her eyes and looked out at the silver-glazed snow. When she spoke her voice seemed to come from far off, as if from the distance of our childhood. 'I remember I was kept away from you. What you had was very contagious and for weeks I couldn't come near you, or Mother, or your nurse, because they might have been carrying the disease on their clothes and hands. It was only dangerous if you were a child, you see. I could hear you coughing through the walls. And there was this funny sound you'd make right at the end of a bout of coughing. You'd be completely out of breath so you'd have to take a big gulp of air and it sounded like a *whoop*.'

That sounded like the hundred-day cough, I thought. Whooping cough! Children died from it all the time in Amentia, and there was absolutely nothing about the disease that could turn a person's eyes ice-blue and their hair black.

I sat back. 'Thanks,' I whispered.

Lilith shrugged and closed her eyes.

I looked at Renata, still sound asleep. If it wasn't the hundred-day cough that had made me like I was, then what was she hiding from me?

'Fina,' Lilith said, using my childhood nickname. 'Don't take this the wrong way, but I've always had the feeling that you're a bit different from us. Me and Mother, I mean. The sickness changed your colouring, but . . . It's something else. I think . . . I think you see a different world to us. And because you see a different world it makes *you* a bit different.' Lilith looked at me warily, as if worrying she'd upset me. 'Not necessarily in a bad way,' she added hastily. 'Do you feel . . .?' She trailed off.

Did the sickness change me on the inside,

she was asking. 'Different?' I asked.

She nodded, regarding me closely.

This was my chance. I could tell her what I'd been hiding all these years. That I was afraid of myself and what I might do. What I could turn into. How scared I was. But how could I tell her that I dreamt of drinking blood, and that in my dreams I liked it?

'No,' I said, shaking my head. 'No different at all.'

———

Closer to Pergamia, the dreams got worse. One recurred nearly every night.

I was in a dark place, like a bedroom in the small hours of the morning, and there was something in my mouth. It was metallic, warm and rich.

Blood.

I held something warm to my lips, and the blood filled my mouth over and over, and I swallowed greedily. It was the most delicious and reviving liquor, and I couldn't get enough.

Finally, the flow stopped, and I realised what I was holding. It was an arm. Lilith's arm.

I had opened her wrists to drink her blood. And I had drained her dry.

———

As the weather grew warmer, Mother and Lilith grew animated and excited. Once we crossed into Pergamia, they were unbearable.

I, on the other hand, could only feel an overwhelming sense of trepidation as the dream grew stronger. I smiled, tight-lipped, as they exclaimed over the green fields and the beautiful flowers. I agreed, 'Yes, aren't they *lovely*,' but I just couldn't rustle up any enthusiasm.

Occasionally I saw the blue-eyed phantom on the edge of my dreams as I was tortured with images of death and blood. Once, I woke in the middle of the night and saw twin blue points of light travelling next to the coach, but before I could yank the window down and have a proper look it had disappeared. *Give me back my ring!* I had called in my mind, but had heard nothing in reply. I began to fear the night and the dreams it would bring.

The morning we were to arrive at the palace, Renata snapped. 'Why are you constantly moping, Zeraphina? Do you not like the beautiful sunny days, the fresh fruit and the stunning scenery? Are you wishing you were back in that cold, run-down castle of ours?'

I straightened in my seat and tried to look happy. 'No, Mother. I am tired of the journey, that is all. I haven't been sleeping well.' I glanced at Lilith. 'And I've been thinking how lonely I shall be in Amentia with Lilith gone.' I winced inwardly at my lie. Of course, that's what should have been making me miserable, if I wasn't so wrapped up in myself.

Lilith smiled and patted my hand. 'Oh, Fina.'

Renata sat back, satisfied. 'Yes, of course. As shall I. But don't worry. As soon as we get home there'll be no end of suitors calling for you. Lilith's advantageous marriage is going to make you quite a catch, young lady,' she assured me with a smile.

I groaned inwardly. Suitors. Something to look forward to.

'Now,' she said briskly, 'wipe that mopey look off your face. We'll be arriving at any moment and you need to look happy to be here. Lean forward and let me fix your hair.'

She pulled the curls Eugenia had set that morning into a soft halo round my face. We were all dressed in the Pergamian style: loose, toga-like gowns that were belted around the waist with braiding. The seams along the tops of the arms weren't closed up, but instead attached at regular intervals by strips of fabric. The style showed our slender shoulders off to advantage and the dresses were very cool. They needed to be; the midday sun was fierce. Not used to it, we had taken to fanning ourselves with our books.

Xallentaria was bordered with fortifications, and as we crossed into the city proper I saw many soldiers patrolling the area and posted atop walls, their keen eyes trained on the sky and bows at the ready. What sort of enemy came from above? I looked up, but didn't see anything except a vaulted blue sky.

On the shimmering horizon, beyond the domes and spires of the city, the palace rose, robust and proud, and gleaming in the midday sun.

Despite the presence of the soldiers the cityfolk looked cheerful enough and bustled about their business. There were women in gowns like our own. In twos and threes they sat under tea-house awnings, sipping from coloured glasses and nibbling sweets from tiny platters. Merchants plied their wares and children ran all over, playing tag and eliciting lazy calls from their parents to behave. Girls the same age as Lilith and me wandered here and there, holding parasols to protect their complexions and gossiping behind lacy fans.

The palace lay on the north-eastern side of the city at the end of a long, tree-lined boulevard. Lilith and I hung out the carriage windows and gawked at it until Renata dragged us back.

'Act unimpressed,' she told us. 'You're supposed to be princesses for goodness' sake, not country bumpkins.'

I sat back, but tilted my head so I could see out the window. Everything was made of white stone and hurt the eyes to look at. The main keep, in which would be the great hall and living quarters of the king and queen and those at court, rose far above the outer walls, an immaculate, gleaming structure. I counted eighteen turrets, capped with gold and flying the nation's blue-and-gold standard.

It made our own castle look like an outhouse.

I'd been expecting grand and ostentatious, but this was something else. This was splendour, and magnificence, and more than a little imposing.

'Oh, dear,' Lilith moaned, clutching her stomach and turning green. 'I don't feel very well. We *are* bumpkins, Mother. What am I even doing here?'

Renata, alarmed, began fanning her with a book. 'Nonsense, Daughter. It's just nerves. See how beautiful you look today? The air agrees with you.'

The palace's outer walls were patrolled by soldiers marching along the wide stone parapets. We passed through the gates and into beautiful gardens with sweeping lawns. Wandering among the rich green foliage I saw a beautiful blue-and-green bird that made strange, sad cries. As we passed, it turned and regarded us with a regal gaze. Then its trailing golden tail rose and spread like a fan to reveal a hundred eyes.

Our little procession came to a halt within an enormous courtyard. The door of the carriage was opened by a footman, and Lilith and I stood blinking in the immense space, gazing up at the four white walls around us. The place was enormous. It was also empty except for soldiers posted at intervals along the walls and around the bailey. There was no welcoming ceremony, no fanfare. I looked around for the servants' carriage and our guards but it seemed they had been diverted elsewhere. I wondered where Leap and Griffin were.

'Why is there no one to meet us?' Lilith asked.

Anxiety passed over Renata's features. This clearly wasn't a good sign.

Lilith began to look green again.

From across the courtyard a very handsomely dressed man approached, nose raised to the sky. He walked straight up to Renata and bowed from the waist until his back was completely level with his hips. He righted himself, and in a voice altogether too loud given we were standing quite close, he announced, 'Your Majesty, Your Royal Highnesses, welcome to the House of Pergamia. The king and queen hope that you had a swift and agreeable journey.' He gave a half bow and held out an arm, indicating that we should follow him. 'Your chambers await.' He led us through the main entrance – 'Thank goodness we're not going in the tradesmen's door,' hissed Renata – which was huge and grand like the rest of the palace. It was bordered with tall marble columns and the floor was laid with more marble. I realised the reason for it once we were inside. As well as being ornamental, the marble was blessedly cool. We were led up grand, sweeping staircases and along airy landings dotted with suits of armour and portraits of the relations. Portly women and bearded men abounded, all looking quite plain and severe. I hoped, for Lilith's sake, that Amis had fared better.

As soon as we were alone in our apartment, a suite of three bed chambers with a shared living room, Lilith and I flopped onto couches. She smiled at me wearily. We had arrived.

Renata paced, reading the rooms like a gypsy poring over a palm. 'The bedrooms face west, which gives a good view of the city, but I'm not altogether sure that they are the best in the palace – not counting the king and queen's, of course. The beds are entirely too small, and I'm really not sure about the size of this living room.'

It was far grander than anything we had at home. On the rose-streaked marble floor stood a low table, bordered by three ample couches and loaded with plush cushions. In a raised alcove we had a breakfast table with a huge bowl of exotic fruits on it, and around the walls were some beautiful artworks: delicately painted silk screens, ornate candelabra and the most delicate china vases.

'Perhaps I misjudged the importance of our visit,' Renata fretted. She paced back and forth, eyeing the vases ('elegant'), the plasterwork on the ceiling ('ornate'), and the paintings ('ugly, but expensive-looking'). Fingering the silk curtains that led to an enormous sunny terrace, she pronounced, 'Well, we're not ridiculously important, but we're not embarrassingly lowly either.' She sniffed. 'It will have to do.'

I rolled my eyes. What was she going to do, march out and demand a room change?

We sat under the awning on the terrace, gulping pomegranate and lime cordial and staring at the view. The whole city was spread out below us, grid-like and with many spires, gardens and ornate buildings. I hoped we would get to go down into the town and walk around. I had never been in such a populous place before and wanted to haggle in the markets over trinkets and eat from street-vendor's stalls.

Before the footman had left our quarters he'd announced that there was to be a reception in our honour that evening. Renata told us that it would be a lengthy affair so we retired to our respective rooms to take an afternoon nap. I was too keyed-up to sleep so I sat on my private balcony, gazing at the city. A servant had somehow got Leap and Griffin into my room, and after greeting me with purrs and squawks they sat and stared at the view with the same wide-eyed wonder as me.

I was here, in the north.

Phantom, do your worst.

FOUR

I eventually dropped off to sleep, but the nap wasn't nearly long enough. Renata was soon shaking me awake. With a bleariness that only comes from sleeping in the afternoon, I dragged myself out of bed and into a steaming bath. As I washed my hair I could see out the balcony door. It was nearing dusk and a thousand little lights had sprung up all over the city. A bath with a view: it was too luxurious. It was also a novelty not to have the bathwater turn icy after only a few minutes. I sniffed the fragrant air, smelling the sea and jasmine flowers growing in the garden.

On the terrace, the last of the sun's rays dried my hair. I combed it into a river of black that cascaded down my back. Looking to the north I saw a sparkle that must be the sea: the Straits of Unctium. Beyond that must be Lharmell, invisible over the horizon. I wondered how far it was. How long it would take to get there by seacraft.

Renata and Eugenia were both tending to Lilith so I dressed myself in the metallic silver gown laid out for me. Then I sat in the living room twisting my one silver ring on my thumb and wondering when something was going to happen. I was impatient for it, my stomach hovering high in my chest with anticipation and fear.

Lilith was cranky and didn't want to be bothered with hot-irons for her hair or pots of rouge for her lips and cheeks. Batting the women away, she said, 'Oh, what's the bother? The servant said it would just be a little celebration.'

Renata caught her daughter's chin in her hand. 'This will be the first time you are to meet Prince Amis. Tonight will be almost as big as your wedding feast, you silly girl.'

Lilith pulled away. 'Then why did he say it?' she asked sulkily.

'Because,' Renata said, 'in court, a "little celebration" is code for a great big fuss! Now stand still.'

When she'd done with Lilith, Renata stood us side by side in front of a large mirror. 'Look at yourselves, my beautiful girls,' she whispered.

We looked, and never before had I been more aware of the difference between us. Lilith was in a gown of the purest white, and her red-gold hair was curled delicately round her face. In contrast, my hair and dress shone darkly, and black kohl around my eyes made me look quite striking. Pointing first at my reflection and then at her own, Lilith said in surprise, 'You look like the moon, and I look like the sun.'

I saw that she was right. We were two sides of the same coin: she of the day and I of the night. It felt like an omen. I recalled the black forest and a shiver of trepidation ran down my spine.

'Did you do this on purpose?' Lilith asked Renata.

Renata was fiddling with her hair in the mirror. 'Of course, darling. Everyone's going to see how different the two of you are anyway, so it's best to emphasise it now rather than let them think I'm trying to cover up a bastard child.'

But was she? The question burned in my mind. What else could explain the way I looked?

I felt a warm body press against my leg and bent to see luminous green eyes looking up at me. Having been parted from me for such an exceptional length of time, Leap and Griffin were both adamant they were coming to dinner. I tried to coax them back to my room, but Renata said, to my surprise, 'No, take your little pets with you. They're quite strange-looking and might impress the court.'

'Really?'

Renata looked to the heavens. 'When will you girls start to realise that in these matters, I know best?'

I ran to get my gauntlet before she could change her mind. While I was fastening it on, Renata tutted and said, 'It does quite ruin the outfit, though.'

A liveried footman led us through labyrinthine corridors to the great hall. Suddenly struck by nerves, Lilith took my arm. 'What if he's an absolute troll?' she hissed, looking warily at Renata's back.

'Well,' I whispered, 'either you marry him and have a tribe of little trolls, or you'll have to fake your own death. Because Mother's not letting you get out of this alive, is she?'

Lilith gave me a tense glance and shook her head. She was looking slightly green again.

We arrived at a huge set of ornate doors. From behind them we could hear the chatter of what sounded like hundreds of people.

The doors swung open, revealing a cavernous space hung with crystal chandeliers. It was filled with guests, all talking and laughing loudly, and so far oblivious to our presence.

A panicked thought flashed through my mind. We might stand like this all night, completely ignored. What if the king and queen had forgotten they'd even sent for us? It had taken us weeks to get here.

I saw my own fears echoed threefold on Lilith's face, and for an instant I was afraid she was going to turn tail and run.

The footman stepped forward. He held a staff that he banged on the marble floor three times. It made a sound like the tolling of a bell, and echoed around the room. Everyone fell silent and hundreds of faces turned to us in unison. Never in my life had I been in a room with so many people, all looking towards me at once.

There was a strained moment when no one moved, and then, as one, the court dipped into curtseys and bows, the only noise the rustle of the women's satin dresses.

'His Royal Highness, Prince Amis of Pergamia,' the footman bellowed.

The crowd parted, and pacing towards us was a golden-haired young man. He was pale and slender like many of the other men in the room, but had a jaunty step and a twinkle in his eye. Not a troll. Rather handsome, in fact, and not daunting in the slightest.

I heard Lilith let out the breath she'd been holding.

The prince smiled and held out his hands to Renata, clasping hers in his. 'It *is* a pleasure to meet you, my queen. And your lovely daughters.' His eyes flashed to Lilith, a smile curving his lips.

Renata inclined her head. 'And it is a great pleasure to meet you, Prince Amis. May I present my eldest daughter, Princess Lilith?'

'Indeed you can,' he exclaimed. He took Lilith's hand, bowing over it and kissing it with some enthusiasm. 'My lady,' he said. There was a look in his eyes as he regarded Lilith, intense and responsive. I think he liked what he saw.

'And may I present my youngest daughter, Princess Zeraphina.'

Amis reached for my hands and seemed to notice for the first time that there was an eagle perched on one of them. With her glittering black eyes and sharp beak, it was difficult for others to tell the difference between Griffin being friendly and Griffin about to strike. I, on the other hand, could tell she was in a very good mood.

'Oh – ah, hello,' he said to me, taking back his hands. His smile faltered and he settled for a little nod. Then he jumped. Leap was curling around his ankles, gazing up at the prince and purring audibly. Amis tried to step away from his coiling body but Leap was quite insistent with his affection. He was leaving silvery hair on the prince's white stockings.

'What nice, erm, pets,' Amis said, still trying to step out of Leap's way.

'Thank you, your highness,' I said. 'Leap,' I hissed, and he made his way back to my side.

Amis took Lilith's arm and said to all of us, 'Do come and meet my parents. I know they're dying to meet you.'

We paced through the crowd, all eyes on us. I drew quite as many stares as Lilith. All were in full court dress, the women in floaty silk gowns much like our own, the men in well-cut trousers and frothy shirts. Coiffures were not limited to the ladies; it seemed that in Pergamia the men liked to dress as fancifully as their partners.

Across an expanse of blue-and-gold carpet, the king and queen were seated on their thrones. Behind them hung the Pergamian standard, a hefty golden sword on a blue background. The king had a more-salt-than-pepper beard and the queen was a little on the dumpy side, rather like the portraits of past Pergamian royals. They were dressed in golden robes and very heavy-looking crowns, and their eyes were fixed on a point somewhere above our heads. They seemed rather aloof, but as we neared they broke into friendly smiles. To their left stood a girl, grinning at us. She had curly blonde hair like Amis's and I guessed she was his sister.

At the king's right hand was a dark-haired man about Amis's age. He had his hands clasped behind his back and watched our approach gravely. I found he drew my gaze, and he was conspicuous not only by his simple attire of black trousers and white shirt, but the way he held himself; with strength and pride. With his broad shoulders and strong features he made the other men in their powdered wigs and lacy cravats seem slight and silly. I saw his eyes widen as he regarded first Leap, then Griffin, and then me. I thought good manners would make him look away, but he kept staring. My cheeks grew hot, and I wondered what he thought gave him the right to look so candidly at me.

A herald with a long feather in his cap stepped forward. He blew a horn and, in a pealing voice, began to make the introductions. 'Their Majesties King Askar and Queen Ulah, rulers of the House of Pergamia, Saviours of Brivora and Protectors of the Free World.'

I resisted the urge to raise my eyebrows at such a

lavish introduction. It seemed Their Royal Majesties had high opinions of themselves.

The herald continued. 'Her Royal Highness Princess Carmelina, Daughter of the House of Pergamia.'

Carmelina curtseyed, and a smile dimpled her features.

'The Honourable Rodden Lothskorn.'

The dark-haired man lowered his head in what barely passed as a bow. He clearly wasn't one of the family, but was being introduced as if he was as important as any of them. As he raised his head he caught me staring, and my eyes snapped back to the king.

The herald took a huge breath and cried, 'Presenting Her Majesty Queen Renata Octavia, ruler of the House of Amentia.' Renata stepped forward and dropped into a low curtsey which she held for several moments.

Where were our lengthy titles? Something like Presumptuous Ones from the Poorest Nation in the Land, or Desperate Ones of the Freezing Country would be fitting.

'Princess Lilith Oriana, First Daughter of the House of Amentia.' Lilith stepped forward to stand beside Renata and dropped into a very graceful curtsey. All eyes were on her, but she kept her serenity.

'Princess Zeraphina Hermione, Second Daughter of the House of Amentia.'

Oh, golly. My turn. I checked that Griffin was settled securely on my wrist and that Leap hadn't wandered off and together we stepped forward. Carmelina's eyes grew round as saucers when she saw my animals. I curtseyed, wobbled, and Griffin had to flap her wings to keep her balance. Leap was staring at the king and queen with big green eyes. I hoped he wasn't about to disgrace us by climbing the tapestries or, worse, washing his rear end. As I rose from my curtsey I saw Rodden Lothskorn raise an eyebrow, looking at my black hair. Then he glanced at Mother, then Lilith, then back at me, a question in his eyes. I felt my indignation rise. I could tell exactly what he was thinking, and even though I wondered it myself, he had no right.

'What a pleasure it is to have you all here,' King Askar boomed. 'We hope your stay with us will be to your liking, and you will have many, many reasons to return.' He smiled meaningfully at Lilith, and I saw the prince duck his head to hide a blush of pleasure.

Was it really to be this easy? Were we simply to arrive, and the deal was done?

In the midst of all the pleasant, smiling faces I caught sight of Lothskorn's. He wasn't smiling. I saw the muscles bunching in his jaw.

'Thank you, my king,' Renata said, curtseying again. Lilith and I hastily followed.

'We are to have a little supper in your honour,' trilled the queen, 'and I do look forward to hearing all about you, my dears.'

Everyone broke rank and relaxed. Everyone, that was, except me. Even Lilith looked calm, gazing at Prince Amis like she'd never heard of Lester of Varlint. Out of the corner of my eye I could see Rodden Lothskorn regarding me, looking like he'd swallowed a lemon. I wondered if he was about to have a quiet word in the king's ear – call off the betrothal due to the suspected illegitimacy of the queen's youngest daughter.

My cheeks burned. If he said one word about me to the king I would sic Griffin onto him, court be damned.

The doors to the dining hall opened. The court musicians struck up a fanfare. Again, 'little supper' was a gross understatement. The high table was festooned with brass terrines, towering monuments of fruit, meats in aspic, and loaves of bread that resembled sculptures. The trestles below all but groaned under the weight of similar dishes, plus rows and rows of golden cups filled with wine and mead.

I saw Amis offer his arm to Lilith. A man in a sea-green jacket and fingers filled with gold rings approached me, ready to lead me to dinner, but to my annoyance, Rodden Lothskorn cut in front of him and offered me his arm.

'Your Highness,' he murmured.

I hesitated for a second and he cleared his throat meaningfully, insisting that I take his arm.

I fumed, but Renata was watching me so I threaded my hand through his proffered elbow.

As he led me through to dinner, I sneaked a closer look at him from beneath my lashes. His dark brows were drawn down in a most unpleasant expression, introspective and somewhat displeased. It was clear he took no pleasure in my company. Why offer his arm if he didn't want to, and didn't seem to have any intention of talking to me? It made no sense. Then I remembered what Renata had said about protocol. Maybe it was written in stone that arrogant jerks had to lead the younger sisters of future queens of the nation through to dinner.

It was rather hard on younger sisters, I thought.

Wordlessly, he led me to the high table and seated himself beside me. Amis was on my other side. Leap had already wandered off but Griffin settled herself on the back of my chair so she could glower at the room in general. The court took their seats at the lower table, and a buzz of chatter started up as the first inches were drained from the wine cups. It felt very strange to be at the dinner table with a crowd seated below us, as if we were actors in a play. I was aware that, while Lilith was drawing most of the stares, I was getting a few as well. I could well imagine what they were saying.

Look at the little bastard with the animals.

Servants began dishing out food from silver platters. A girl offered me something that looked like a big roasted chicken.

'What is it?' I asked.

'Peacock, Your Highness.'

'What is peacock?'

The girl looked at me strangely.

'A peacock is a bird with a big fancy tail,' Rodden Lothskorn said, helping himself to the roasted meat.

I was reminded of the bird we had seen coming into the grounds. 'Not . . .' I said hesitantly. 'Not the ones that have all the eyes on their tail and sound very sad?'

'That's them.'

I shook my head at the serving girl. 'No, thank you.' They *eat* them? I thought they had just been to look at. I wondered if it could have been the same one I'd admired, and felt a little sick. After that, nothing at the table looked particularly appetising, but I helped myself to something leafy to give the pretence of eating.

'I'm afraid we don't have any mice,' said Rodden, 'but would you like to try some quail?'

I turned to him in surprise. 'I beg your pardon?'

He was holding out a platter of tiny roasted birds to Griffin. 'I was talking to your eagle.'

Griffin's eyes blazed, and then she snatched a quail in her beak and flew off into a dark corner.

There was a trill and Leap jumped into my lap. He'd twigged that food was on offer and he wasn't getting any. I got a bit of miscellaneous meat for him, hoping it wasn't dolphin or unicorn.

Rodden stopped eating and looked at Leap. 'Where did you get a Verapinian drain-cat?'

'A what?'

'A drain-cat from Verapine,' he said.

'Oh, that's much clearer,' I muttered.

He was smiling, looking at Leap, but his eyes flashed to me for a second. The smile changed his whole countenance, and I found myself wishing he'd looked at me the way he was looking at my cat when he'd offered his arm. I might have been rather more disposed to accept it.

'Verapine is very far away,' he said. 'It's a slum country, and drain-cats live in the city's sewage pipes.'

'Sewerage?' I looked at Leap. 'No wonder you left.'

'You can tell by his eyes that he's used to being in the dark,' Rodden continued. 'And water would run right off that silvery coat of his.' He gave Leap's cheek a scratch and, traitorously, Leap purred and closed his eyes.

What an odd man. Not three words to me, but he goes all gooey over a lady's pet. The look that had come into his eyes as he'd spoken of Verapine had been one of true affection, as if he knew the place well. There was something foreign to his countenance; the planes of his face were broader and more sculpted than the narrow, soft faces of the northern Brivorans, and the combination of dark hair and olive skin made him stand out in a room full of fair-skinned blonds. It seemed Rodden Lothskorn, as close as he was to the king, wasn't Pergamian at all.

'Where did you get him?' Rodden asked.

I shrugged. 'He just turned up one day. I've had him ever since.'

After regarding me for a moment, he stood. 'Please excuse me,' he said, inclining his head. 'I hope you have a pleasant evening.'

I watched his broad back retreating. He stooped to murmur in the king's ear. My heart leapt into mouth, certain they were speaking of me; but the king merely toasted Rodden with his goblet, and the dark-haired man left the hall without a backward glance.

I had an uneasy feeling that I'd just been subjected to a test, and I wasn't sure if I'd passed or failed.

Next to me, Amis was engrossed in Lilith, and everyone else was too far away to start up a conversation with. Even the serving girls skipped over me, and I spoke to no one for the rest of the dinner.

'He's falling for you,' Renata said to Lilith as we made our way back to our rooms. The two walked side by side, hands clasped in excitement.

'Do you really think so?'

'Oh, yes, darling. He didn't talk to anyone else all night.'

I rolled my eyes. Tell me about it.

'I'm going to bed,' I said as soon as we entered

our apartment, not that they noticed. I closed my door on their twittering and stood on my balcony. I could feel the blood-hunger humming in the recesses of my mind. My eyes searched the northern sky, yearning for something, like a bird with her wings clipped.

It was a clear night, but very dark. I watched the stars, too keyed-up to sleep. I was looking at a constellation when I saw, from right to left, a group of stars wink out, and then reappear.

That was strange. I studied the sky harder. I saw nothing for a few minutes, and then I saw it again: a group of stars disappeared and then reappeared. It was a while before I realised what was happening. Something was passing in front of the stars, blocking out their light. Whatever it was moved too fast to be cloud. Leap had his paws up on the ledge and was staring at the sky. He saw it too.

The wind picked up and then all over the sky stars were winking on and off. A whisper of song reached my ears. It grew louder, and I recognised it as the same keening I had heard in my not-dream the night before we left Amentia. I leaned out from the balcony, craning my neck for a better view. From below and above, I heard running feet and hushed, urgent shouts: soldiers. They seemed to be reacting as if to an attack, but as quietly as possible so as not to disturb the sleeping castle. I saw the outline of an archer atop a wall, his bow and arrow trained on the heavens.

Moving to my chamber door, I listened. There was no sound from without so I inched it open. All clear. I sneaked out of the apartment and into the corridor, intent on getting to the northern parapet. I slipped along the landings, keeping to the shadows. Leap paced beside me, silent on his velvet paws.

I searched for a doorway that would lead upwards. I found one, and hurried up a spiral staircase that I hoped led to the battlements and not up a turret. After a few turns I came out into the parapet. I kept to the shadows, not wanting to attract the attention of a soldier with a loaded bow.

I could tell from the alignment of the stars that my sense of direction was right: I was at the northernmost part of the keep. Forty yards away was the turret closest to Lharmell, the topmost arrow slot gleaming with a sickly orange light. I wondered if it could be a beacon of some sort for the Lharmellins. But that would make whoever was responsible for the light a traitor to Pergamia.

The wind dropped suddenly and the singing died away, replaced by the earthly mutterings of soldiers.

The sky had emptied and they were going back to their posts. I peeled myself out of the shadows and left the parapet, casting one last longing look at the stars.

Back in my room, I crawled under the mosquito netting that hung over my bed, Leap burrowing in with me. From a chest of drawers, Griffin ruffled her feathers in her sleep. She, stuffed full of quail, hadn't woken.

Long into the night I watched for the twin blue glows that would announce my ghostly visitor, but they never came.

FIVE

'Good morning!' Lilith cried, flinging my bedroom door open.

I knew that tone: she was unbearably, infuriatingly in love. I threw the bedclothes over my face. 'You didn't take long,' I muttered.

'To what? Get up? It's nearly mid-morning, sleepyhead.'

I heard her go to the window and, with relish, take a deep breath of Pergamian air.

'Had sweet dreams about princey, did we?'

Lilith flounced over and sat on my bed. 'Oh, Fina, he's perfect! So handsome and so charming.'

'A handsome and charming prince. How very original of him.'

She poked me in the side. 'Why are you so grumpy

this morning? Look, it's gorgeous outside.' She ran to the balcony again.

'Ow,' I said, rubbing my side and emerging from swathes of netting.

'Amis is going to take us on a tour of the grounds this morning.'

'Oh, goody.' I would have to watch while they canoodled in the arbours.

At the breakfast table Renata poured me a glass of something orange.

'It's orange juice,' she said.

'I can see that,' I muttered, swiping my hair out of my eyes. 'What if I want red juice, or blue juice?'

'It's not named for its colour, you silly girl. It's named after the fruit. *Oranges.*' She pointed at something round and, funnily enough, orange, in the fruit bowl. 'Now drink up. Carmelina can't wait to get to know you.'

I drained my glass. Carmelina. That would be the cheerful blonde girl from the night before. She looked perky and excitable, two things I wasn't in the mood for. What on earth would we talk about? Boys? But then again, Carmelina might know something about Lharmell.

They were waiting for us down in the courtyard. Amis offered Lilith his arm and they smiled at each other with sunny faces. I walked beside Carmelina, a girl whose step was as bouncy as her hair.

'Wasn't last night absolutely boring?' she asked, as the four of us strolled out the gates and into the grounds.

'Very,' I said.

'Being at high table is like being an animal in a zoo. Everyone always stares and it puts me off my food. I thought I might get to sit next to you, which would have been fun, but then Rodden took you away to the other end and I had to sit next to your mother. Not that there's anything wrong with your mother! But Rodden's as stiff as a corpse, so I was thinking, poor you. Did he say anything?'

'Not really. He said more to my eagle.'

'Ugh, that's so like him. He never has time for girls.'

We were both holding parasols as the sun was very fierce. Carmelina crossed her eyes to try to look at her nose. 'I think I'm getting freckles. It's not very fashionable to have freckles right now. I wish I had skin like yours. It's like that white stone, what's it again? Ala-something.'

'Alabaster?' I asked.

'Yes, that's the one. Not a single freckle.'

The grounds were even more beautiful on foot. We were following a little winding path and the grass all around was springy and emerald green, dotted here and there with flower beds. We didn't have flowers at our palace. There had been daffodils and bluebells in spring when I was young but they hadn't flowered in a few years. They'd been killed by the frosts.

We passed an idyllic spot with a large sundial bordered with yellow flowers and garden benches. Then there was a fountain spraying jets of water into the clear morning air, with creepers growing up its basin. Amis gave Lilith a coin and she tossed it in, making a wish. Carmelina made a gagging sound. I was inclined to agree with her. There was something distasteful about watching your own sibling court.

'Where are your cat and your bird?' Carmelina asked.

'Eagle,' I corrected. 'Leap is asleep on my bed and Griffin is hunting.' I shaded my eyes against the sun and looked up. There was a speck in the sky over a distant part of the grounds. 'There she is.' The speck suddenly dropped, falling from the sky at an alarming rate. Carmelina gasped, probably wondering if Griffin had just had a heart attack. Then she reappeared, flapping her wings and carrying something in her claws.

'Is she dangerous? I'd be worried she'd peck my eyes out.'

'Certainly not. I'll show you.' I stuck two fingers in my mouth and whistled, making everyone jump. Lilith looked around sharply.

What? I mouthed at her. If she was going to bill and coo like a demented dove, I would make my own fun. Everyone watched as Griffin flew towards my raised arm and settled on my gauntleted wrist, a mouse dangling from her claws.

'Ick,' said Carmelina, eyeing the sharp beak that was presently tearing the little mouse to shreds.

Amis came over. 'Isn't she a beauty!' he said. 'Some of the soldiers hunt with falcons but I've never seen one like this before.'

'She's an eagle,' I said, not even trying to keep the smugness from my voice.

Lilith hung back, grimacing at the gruesome spectacle of my bird gulping down strings of intestine. She glared at me behind Amis's back, so I gave a soft whistle and Griffin flew off.

Patrols were marching through the gardens but they kept their distance from us, being as discreet as soldiers in clanking armour could be. Archers stood atop the surrounding walls, eyes on the horizon.

I waited until Lilith and Amis were a safe distance away before asking, 'You've certainly got a lot of guards. Is it always like this?'

'Oh, yes,' said Carmelina. 'Rodden's orders.'

'Rodden Lothskorn? What has it got to do with him?'

'He's the king's advisor. And Amis's best friend.'

That explained his place at the high table. 'But he's so young,' I protested. I had imagined the king would surround himself with a lot of stuffy yes-men, not take advice from a young man.

'He's twenty-two, I think. But he's very smart. He knows all about the war.' Here, Carmelina coloured up.

'The war?' I asked very casually, admiring a shrub.

Carmelina gave a little laugh. 'Oh, nothing. You know. Grown-up stuff. Very dull. Would you like a peppermint?' She offered me a sweet from a little paper bag.

I sucked on the lolly for a moment, thinking. 'Carmelina, what do you know about Lharmell?'

Carmelina's eyes widened in horror. 'Shh! We're not supposed to talk about that place. They might hear you.'

This was more like it. She did know something, and the way she was reacting, it was juicy, too. Still, I didn't want to appear too eager. 'Who? Lilith and Amis?'

'No,' she said in a whisper. 'The Lharmellins.'

I looked around. 'Are we being spied on?'

Carmelina looked around too, her eyes darting into the shadowy parts of the gardens. 'We could be. Who knows? They've got strange powers.' She gripped my arm, staring into my eyes. 'They're not human.'

I suddenly felt a bit sick. 'Oh, really?' I said, trying to keep my voice light. 'What are they?'

She shrugged. 'I don't know, but they're dangerous. They like blood. You know, to *eat*.'

My mouth dropped open.

Blood. *To eat.*

At the same time as I was revolted, I felt the hunger flare up inside at the mention of blood.

Carmelina saw the horrified expression on my face and nodded. 'I know. It's ghastly, isn't it? But Rodden says we're not to talk about it. We're just to get on with things and he will deal with it. Let's catch up with the others.' She grabbed my hand and tugged me along, as if we could leave our conversation behind like a bit of unappealing scenery.

The events at dinner suddenly took on a whole new meaning. I remembered the cold looks Rodden had given me, the suspicion in his eyes. The way he'd looked at me as if I were the enemy. What if I was the enemy – the bastard child of a Lharmellin?

Could my mother have betrayed my father with a monster? She'd lied to me about my illness. Maybe she'd lied about who my father was as well. It would explain my terrible hunger for blood.

I yanked my arm from Carmelina's grasp. 'Why are you at war with the Lharmellins? What have they done?'

Carmelina shot a glance at me, nodding surreptitiously towards Amis and Lilith. 'Oh yes, the ducks are lovely,' she said for their benefit. Then she hissed, 'I'm sorry, I just can't talk about it. Rodden would be very angry with me.'

I spent the rest of the excursion smiling and admiring the ducks, the trees and even more flowers, and looking like I was having a jolly good time. On the inside I was in turmoil. It didn't make sense that Renata would bring me to Pergamia and let me be exposed as one of their enemy. I thought of the king and queen's beaming smiles. They hadn't looked suspicious of me. No one had been anything less than welcoming to me. Except Rodden. There was something about him that I didn't like, and now to find out that he had everybody too scared to even say 'Lharmellin' made me wonder what he was afraid of.

If no one was going to tell me what I needed to know, I would just have to find out myself.

I considered my options, which were few. I had seen Lilith flirt with Lester of Varlint, and that seemed to have got her anything she wanted. If I found the right person and flirted at them, they might start talking in order to show off. Perhaps a soldier. I could go all gooey over his uniform and shoot a few stealthy questions at him.

Later in the afternoon Renata and Lilith had tea with the king and queen and Amis. I suspected, as I hadn't been invited, that it was to discuss the betrothal. I sat on my balcony, tossing an apple back and forth between my hands but not feeling hungry enough to bite into it. Leap sat on my lap, watching dragonflies dance above pots of geraniums. The vivid blooms were beautiful, but I was heartily sick of looking at flowers. Instead, I gazed out over the city. I imagined that the streets were bustling with life. I suddenly longed for anonymity, to be one of the cityfolk buying potatoes or selling bolts of fabric. Anyone but a princess turning into a monster.

I heard Lilith and Renata come back. Carrying Leap with me, I went to my bedroom door. 'How did it go?'

Renata clasped her hands under her chin. She looked at Lilith. 'Do you want to tell her?'

Lilith looked like she could barely contain her excitement. 'We're betrothed, and . . .' she paused for effect, 'the wedding's in *one week!*' She ran to me and clasped her arms around me, not even noticing that she was hugging Leap too.

'One week?' I echoed. 'That doesn't give them much preparation time.' And it wouldn't give me much time to nose around, either. After the wedding I would be packed off home again. That is, if whatever had drawn me here allowed it. I thought of the crippling pain I had felt on the morning of the departure when I'd had second thoughts, and shuddered.

Renata flopped onto a settee. 'Darling,' she said. 'They've been making the preparations for weeks. Which is why I knew to have Lilith's dress made before we got here. I told you, Mother knows best.' Her face shone. She loved it when she was right.

I kissed Lilith's cheek. 'I'm very happy for you,' I said, hoping she couldn't see the strain in my eyes. 'I need a lie down. The heat's getting to me.'

I lay beneath the gauzy netting wishing I was back in Amentia practising my archery, and that I had never heard of the blasted north.

Courtly dinners, it seemed, were to be a nightly affair. At the high table that evening I sat next to Carmelina while she chattered at me. She didn't seem to notice that I didn't chatter back. To be fair, if I hadn't had a lot on my mind she might have been a pleasant diversion. But in my present agitated state she was grating on me. I couldn't wait to get away, saying that I needed some fresh air as soon as the meal was over.

The trestles were packed away and I skirted the dancers that were assembling in two rows on the marble floor. I pushed aside the curtains that led to the terrace and stepped into the cool night air.

Music floated on the wind, but it was an earthly tune, coming from the court musicians. I turned and watched the dancers through the gauzy curtains. From where I stood they were an anonymous, homogenised group, whirling and stepping to the smart beat of the tambourine. A nasal horn bleated the melody. Renata had taught me the courtly dances, but I found them rigid. I had imagined a dance to be a fluid thing, open to whim and interpretation. But in fact it was as strict as a military parade. The girls stood in a row on one side, the men on the other, and they moved around in intricate but ordered patterns, now holding hands, now not, passing one another silently. Many of the women held their heads aloof the whole time, bestowing barely a glance on their partner. The whole affair seemed rather cold.

Now would be a good time to make my escape, but as I emerged back into the hall I ran straight into Rodden. I moved to side-step him, but he bowed. You can't walk away when someone's bowing at you, so I waited for him to straighten.

'May I have the next dance?' The words were colourless, automatic; it was barely a question. It was manners making him ask an unpartnered girl to dance. My refusal would be gratefully accepted.

'No, sir, I mean to –'

'As the sister of the bride you should be dancing,' he interrupted. 'If the king thinks you're not enjoying yourself he will begin to wonder if you doubt Pergamia is good enough for your sister, and if the marriage should take place at all. You don't want that, do you?'

For heaven's sake, it was just a dance. 'Indeed not, but . . .'

Rodden held out his hand as if my reply had been an assent. The next dance was beginning. He gave me a hard look. Perhaps it would be safer to go along with it; it might add authenticity to my pretence of being a normal human girl and not the offspring of their blood-drinking enemy. If that's really what I was. I swept past him, ignoring his hand, and took my place. Rigid and cold, I thought. That's what the dances were and that's what I would be.

But the dance wasn't rigid like I'd imagined. As my feet paced well-rehearsed steps, I found there were too many opportunities for glances, intimations. Every touch and turn held meaning and promise. I realised I'd had it all wrong. The ladies weren't aloof, they were coquettish.

Rodden and I stepped towards each other, raising our right hands to take the other's. We turned, our clasped hands a pivot. There were not many places to look. Most couples gazed into each other's eyes, but I couldn't bring myself to do that. I was terrified I was about to give myself away. I stared at our joined hands, my fingers intertwined with his. At last, after eight beats that had seemed like an eternity, we unclasped and paced in a wide arc, moving up the row. The dance was a continuous one, everyone repeating the movements until the line had cycled through once. As we came together again, Rodden murmured, 'Are you counting the beats in your head?'

'No. Why?'

'You look like you're concentrating very hard.'

Yes, on not giving myself away to *you*. 'I've never danced this one before, not properly.'

'I would never have guessed.' His voice was level and I couldn't tell if he was being sincere or sarcastic.

I had resolved that it was safer to keep my mouth shut, but I couldn't help myself. I had just one week in Pergamia and I suddenly felt a burning desire to show this trumped-up politician that, while he might be able to terrify his own people into silence, he didn't scare me.

'My cat saw something in the sky last night,' I said, hoping he wouldn't guess this was a half-truth. Leap had seen it, but I'd seen it first. 'He kept staring, but I couldn't see anything. It was so dark.'

'Bats,' he said curtly.

'Oh. The soldiers started making an awful racket. Are they scared of bats?'

'Hardly.'

We parted for a moment, turned away, turned in again, then reclasped our hands and circled in the other direction.

'Her Majesty the Queen is terrified of bats and has given orders to shoot them down. A fool's errand.'

'Oh, I see.'

The dance ended and he bowed to me. I dropped into a curtsey and before I could rise he had stridden off.

Carmelina was instantly at my side. 'Was that Rodden? He never dances, never ever.'

'I'm honoured,' I said through gritted teeth. 'He didn't want to, you know. It was stupid protocol that made him ask.' Over Carmelina's shoulder I saw Queen Ulah disappear onto the terrace with her husband, laughing and talking as she went. A woman terrified of bats wouldn't go into the open air at night. 'Carmelina, is your mother afraid of bats?'

She gave me an odd look. 'Bats? No. What makes you ask?'

'Oh, nothing. Shall we get some water?' I turned and saw Rodden watching us. His eyes burned with anger – he'd seen me question Carmelina.

The irony was that even though it had been him doing the lying, I was the one in trouble: he knew I was on to him, and that could only make things all the more dangerous for me.

SIX

I started my detective work the very next morning.
Questioning Rodden had been a mistake, but
it wasn't one I was going to make twice. There
were hundreds of people in this castle who must
know something and so far I had barely talked to
any of them.

I scrunched my hair as it dried, making it look
rumpled as if I'd just gotten out of bed. I had a pink
off-the-shoulder gown that made me look a bit like a
dessert, and I put a geranium behind my ear. Feeling
quite ridiculous, I applied a little rouge to my lips
and practised smiling flirtatiously and batting my
eyelashes in the mirror.

There were archery ranges in the bailey and, as
I was feeling a little rusty, it would be a good place

to practise as well as meet a few soldiers. I left Leap curled up on my bed and didn't put on my gauntlet, wanting to appear like any other court lady. But that begged the question: did court ladies practise archery? Never mind, the plan would have to do. It was the only one I had.

The range was deserted when I arrived, so I shot a few arrows for myself. There were all perfect shots; it seemed I wasn't rusty after all. I was yanking the arrows out of the board when I heard a few deep male voices. Four soldiers came onto the range, jostling each other and kicking up dust.

'Right, you lot!' bellowed one of the men. 'Show me you're not a bunch of little girlies and give me some bullseyes.' He looked at me and winked. I forced myself to smile back. Judging from the decorations on his uniform he was the captain, and as I paced back to my firing spot I let my body go languid, trying for a sexy, swaying walk but certain I just looked boneless. I clutched my bow awkwardly, notched up an arrow, pulled back with a deliberately weak arm and fired. The arrow bounced off the target and fell into the dust. I giggled and stomped my foot. Then I rolled my eyes and played with my hair. Was it too much?

A few of the soldiers guffawed.

I notched up another arrow, and as I drew back on the string I shut my eyes and turned my face away as if I was scared to look.

'Here, here, here,' the captain said, coming over. He held out a meaty hand for the bow. Testing the string he said, 'Why, this is a big bow for such a li'l lady. You should 'ave something for your weight class.'

Idiotically, I'd brought my own bow with me. It was large and obviously for a man. My arms had grown rather strong over the years – stronger than they probably should have, no matter how much archery practice I'd done.

I gave the soldier a vacant look.

'You need something smaller, honey,' he explained.

'Oh?' I said, fluttering my lashes at him. 'I had no idea.' I saw a gooey look come into his eyes.

'Well, you'll just have to sort that out later, lovey. But meanwhile, you're gripping it all wrong. Let me show you.'

From behind, he put his arms around me and the bow in my grasp. He smelt vile, like sour wine and unwashed clothes, and his stubble scratched my cheek, but I kept an inane smile on my face. Together we notched up an arrow, drew back and fired. The arrow sank into the board, albeit at the very edge.

'There!' he said, beaming at me. 'Now, that wasn't so hard, was it?'

I twirled the bow in my hands. 'Why, not at all, sir. You soldiers are certainly very . . . capable,' I said, letting my eyes linger over his uniform. Inside his armour, the captain puffed up like a popinjay. I looked around, up at the soldiers on the parapets. 'This palace seems to be so heavily guarded,' I continued. 'Why is that?'

'Why, now, you're not to concern yourself with such things, lovey. You just let Hoggit take care of it.'

Hoggit. The name was as endearing as his face. I twirled a strand of hair in my fingers, forcing myself to look up at him wide-eyed. 'But we're not in any danger, are we? What with the war and all?'

'No, honey, no. Them dirty Lharmellins –'

'Captain Hoggit,' an imperious voice called from the entrance to the range. 'Is there something you should be doing, or would you like me to find something for you?'

Rodden Lothskorn. I dropped the hair I was twirling and folded my arms angrily. Just when I was about to discover something useful.

'Ah, yessir. Going right now. Men!' Hoggit

bellowed, and his soldiers fell in behind him and moved out.

Rodden strolled over to me, hands behind his back. His eyes took in the reddened lips, the tousled hair. My cheeks started to burn. I itched to tug at the neckline of my gown, to pat down my hair.

'I've been watching you. That was either quite a performance or you're a terrible archer.'

'Oh, I don't know,' I said, keeping my voice languid. I notched up an arrow and fired. The arrow sank into the very centre of the target. 'What do you think?'

Rodden looked at the arrow, then at me. His eyes bored into mine as though he could see straight through me. He took the bow from me, weighing it in his hands and testing the string.

Damn, damn, damn! I really should have found a ladies' bow.

'Your hair. Those eyes,' he said, and I could tell he wasn't referring to my make-up. 'This bow. That shot. Your questions. Don't think I haven't noticed.' He handed back the bow. 'I'll be watching you.'

I wasn't going to let him see that he'd rattled me. 'I'm looking forward to it,' I said, and swept past him, putting a little waggle in my step. This flirting thing wasn't so hard after all.

'Don't be a tart,' he called.

My face burned, but I forced myself to continue across the bailey without changing my walk. As soon as I was inside the keep I dropped my bow and pressed my back against the cold, stone wall. Damn him! Was I ever going to find out anything useful?

———

Rodden had left me no choice. Questions weren't getting me anywhere. I would have to snoop.

But what with endless dinners, toasts and high teas to celebrate Amis and Lilith's betrothal, I found it difficult to get away. I was constantly stuffed with food, plied with cordials and wines and surrounded by tedious people. Nobody seemed to know anything about the war, or they just weren't telling. Didn't they care that it was going on right over their heads?

I was sitting within a gaggle of Amis's aunts. All they wanted to talk about was the bride and stuff themselves with tiny pink cakes. After refusing a third glass of wine because I was starting to feel tipsy, I gazed around at the sitting room. It was pink and frilly and belonged to Queen Ulah's sister, Rupa, who lived at court year-long. Rupa was onto her fourth glass and becoming quite cheerful indeed. She and her sisters, Calli and Munah, were discussing the men at court and ranking them in order of attractiveness.

'The Earl of Federna!' shrieked Calli. 'Now there's a man you can hold on to.'

'Yes, all three hundred pounds of him. Honestly, dear, must you always choose the fatties?' said Munah, shoving another cream cake into her jowls.

'Oh, let her have the fatties. More young and handsome ones for the rest of us, eh?' Rupa nudged her neighbour, which set the others off and I found I was being hit repeatedly in the ribs by corpulent elbows.

'Speaking of young and handsome,' continued Rupa, 'how about that strapping Lothskorn fellow? You know, the prince's friend.'

The other aunts clapped and screeched their agreement. I hid a smirk, wondering what Rodden would make of his admirers.

Rupa turned to me. 'You know him. I saw you sitting next to him at high table. What do you think of Lothskorn?'

I considered this. It would be imprudent to say I thought he was devious, rude and untrustworthy, but I was damned if I was going to gush about him to amuse these women. Just remembering the way he'd eyed me on the archery range yesterday as he'd weighed my bow in his hands was enough to make my blood boil. 'He certainly seems committed to keeping the city secure.' There, that was truthful and even mildly complimentary, which was more than he deserved in the circumstances. 'Which reminds me, this war –'

'I like it when he broods!' interrupted Calli.

'He's always brooding,' said Rupa. 'He broods while he eats.'

'But we won't see him tonight, ladies,' said Munah. 'He's off on a little patrol until tomorrow. I told him he'd be sorely missed at dinner tonight, and he gave me the most gentlemanly bow. For all he's a commoner, he cuts a finer figure on a horse than any other man at court.'

Away until tomorrow? That gave me an idea. Now all I needed to do was extricate myself from the aunts. They were already babbling about some baron, so I stood up and said, 'Nature calls!' They didn't pause for breath as I made my way out.

Rodden's quarters, I'd discovered, were in the northernmost turret and not in the main keep – the same turret I'd seen the orange glow coming from the previous night. Was he signalling to the enemy?

Whether he was a spy or not, there could be all kinds of information about Lharmell in his room: maps, books, military plans. Anything would help.

From the bailey I crept up the stone staircase to the parapet in the dusky light, careful that a patrol had just marched past and disappeared round a corner. I didn't want to run into Hoggit and have to explain what a 'little lady' was doing on the battlements. I hurried along the walkway, feeling giddy from the wine I'd drunk and the strong wind buffeting my body.

I reached the stone archway at the base of the turret, glanced quickly around me, and dashed up the staircase.

I emerged, breathless, in one large room. It was cluttered with Rodden's things: books piled on tables, cloaks flung hastily over chairs, a bed strewn with tangled sheets. Several dirty dishes were piled against one wall, dirty clothes against another. It was evident that he didn't allow the servants up here to clean.

I looked around, wondering where to start. Against one wall was a bench covered in papers and strange-looking instruments. I walked over and picked up a glass beaker filled with a thick orange sludge. I sniffed. It smelt awful, like burnt hair and rotten eggs. There were more beakers blown into bulbous shapes and mounted on metal stands, boxes of strange metals and crystals, and an odd thing about a foot tall with two glass circles at the top. It seemed to be made for looking through. I peeked into the eye-pieces but could see nothing. These were the trappings of a mad alchemist's laboratory. What on earth was he up to?

I heard a rustling sound and turned. There was a rabbit hutch on the floor. Smiling, I knelt down to look at it. Several fluffy brown rabbits were sitting on straw, munching carrots. I poked my finger through the wire to scratch one behind an ear, and the others came hopping over. I would never have guessed that such a serious man as Rodden kept bunnies for pets.

To my horror, I heard someone climbing the stairs. I looked around for a hiding spot, a closet maybe, but there didn't appear to be one. I felt panic rise like a tide in my chest: I was about to be caught in Rodden's room. Then I saw the bed. There was a narrow gap between the frame and the floor. I squeezed myself underneath just moments before whoever it was emerged from the stairwell. I could see only ankle-high but whoever it was wore dusty riding boots and seemed to know his way around. It had to be Rodden. He walked slowly across the room, as if he were bone tired. I willed him to walk right out again, but instead the boots came closer. This was just my dumb luck. He was coming over to the bed. He came right up to it and sat down heavily.

'*Oof.*'

'What the hell –' Rodden leapt up again. He groped under the bed, caught my arm and pulled me bodily out from underneath it. Before I knew it I was on my feet, dangling by my wrist and staring into his blazing eyes.

'You!' he said, practically throwing my arm back at me.

'Ow,' I said, rubbing my wrist.

He looked furious. 'What are you doing in here?'

I suddenly felt very angry with him. He kept popping up at the most inopportune moments. 'You,' I said, pointing a finger right at his nose, 'were supposed to be on patrol.'

He gave a short laugh. 'You conniving little –' He stopped. 'And just what were you doing up here? Snooping, no doubt. You've done nothing but snoop since you got here.' He sniffed, frowning. 'And have you been drinking?'

I deflated a little. I had been hoping he wouldn't notice. What a wonderful impression I was making on him, first as a tart and now as a lush. I was just starting to feel the first pangs of mortification when I noticed something. He'd pulled his cloak and jacket off before he'd sat down on the bed and he stood before me in his shirtsleeves. The shirt was open at the neck revealing a strong brown throat. There was a silver chain around his neck, and something hanging from the chain.

I went still, my eyes fixed on his throat. 'What's that?'

He looked confused for a moment, and his hand went up to his neck.

It was my silver ring. The one the phantom had stolen from my room the night before our departure from Amentia.

He muttered a curse and dropped his head forward.

I took a step back, forgetting the bed was behind me, and I sat down hard. He was the blue-eyed phantom. I should have seen it before. His eyes were the same white-blue as mine.

'What are you?' I whispered.

'What am I?' he repeated, standing over me. 'What are *you*?'

'You were in my room in Amentia. You stole my ring. What the hell is going on?'

Shaking his head, he buttoned the neck of his shirt.

I grabbed his arms. 'You have to tell me! Look at my eyes. They're the same as yours. What did this to me? We're the same, aren't we?'

He shook me off. 'Don't be ridiculous. You're nothing like me.' He paced away, hand to his mouth. He turned back. 'You have to leave.'

I rose. 'No, not until you tell me what's going on.'

'No, I mean go back to Amentia. Right now. Before it's too late.'

'Too late? What are you going to do? What's going to happen here? My sister lives here now – she's going to marry the prince. I have to warn her if it isn't safe.'

'It's you,' he said coldly. 'You're what's going to happen. You're putting us all in danger.'

'You're lying. I haven't done anything. You're just worried I'm going to find out what you're up to.'

'If you really love your sister, you'll leave.'

'If? What do you mean, if? Of course I love my sister.'

He gave a short laugh. 'Now, Zeraphina. We

both know that's a lie. I've been watching you. This wedding is just subterfuge. You've barely been at your sister's side the whole time you've been here. Now, if you go home, I might be convinced that you're innocent in all this. If you don't . . .' He shrugged. 'I won't be held responsible for what happens to you.'

My mouth fell open. He was threatening me.

'What gives you the right to talk to me this way?' My voice sounded shrill and afraid even to my own ears. 'I do love my sister and I'm not going anywhere until Lilith is married.'

He glared at me, considering this. 'Fine. Stay for the wedding, but then you go. No snooping, no questioning the soldiers or anyone else. And you remember, one word from me to the king, and this wedding's off, and you and your sister and your beggar-woman of a mother will have to slink back to the block of ice you call home. But I'd rather not have to resort to such drastic measures. Amis is already besotted with Lilith and there's no reason for him to suffer because of you.' He pointed a finger right at my nose. 'But if I get even a whisper that you've been disobeying my orders . . .' He let the words hang in the air.

I smacked his hand away. 'Give me my ring back.'

'No.'

'Why not?'

'Security.'

I scoffed at that. 'It's a trinket. What use is it to you for security?'

'None of your business. Now, are you going to get out of my room, or am I going to have to talk to the king?'

I pushed past him, fists clenched at my sides. 'You don't scare me with your empty threats. I know you're up to something. So guess what? It's going to be *me* watching *you* from now on.'

A taunting smile curved his lips. 'You won't discover anything.'

'Well, we'll see.' I gave him one final glare before I tore down the stairs. I didn't stop running until I was in my room where I stood, back to the door, shaking uncontrollably.

SEVEN

The next day all I wanted to do was stomp around the grounds and glare up at the northern turret. I had told Rodden I would be watching him, after all, and this was the best plan I had come up with so far. But I wasn't even allowed that luxury. It had been decided that we were to go on a shopping expedition into the city. When I say it had been decided, I mean that Renata had decided and we all had to go along with it. Lilith was very happy to, and so was Carmelina. I was bullied into it.

'Daughter, it's such a nice day, and we haven't seen anything of the city yet.'

It was *such* a nice day. Every day was a nice day in Pergamia, it seemed, and I was beginning to wish for some Amentine gloom. I hadn't slept well the night before. My mind had been haunted with visions of blazing blue eyes staring into mine. I had been hot and restless, and felt claustrophobic inside the mosquito netting over my bed. So I'd paced the room like a caged animal, wishing I could fly out the window as Griffin had done earlier in the evening. Leap had been sprawled on the cold stone floor, belly up, trying to catch a breeze. I'd rubbed him with my foot and tried to think of a plan. Any plan. But I didn't even know where to start. Rodden's threat of calling the wedding off might not have been as hollow as I first thought. Who knew how far his influence went with the king?

We rode down to the markets on horseback flanked by two armed guards. I hadn't been on a horse in years and I clung one-handed to the side-saddle. My other hand was clamped atop my head, keeping my broad-brimmed hat from blowing off in the stiff breeze. The sun was blazing hot and I was taking no chances with my 'alabaster' skin – I could be burnt to a frazzle on a day like this.

The others looked effortless and graceful on their horses, which made me even crankier. Lilith wore a trailing cream gown and rode a smart white horse. In one relaxed hand she held the reins, and the other lay in her lap. She held her head regally and I could see a dreamy look in her eyes that betrayed her private thoughts. I was quite certain she was head over heels in love with Amis, and the whole of Pergamia too. Renata's back was as straight as a ramrod and her triumphant expression was befitting one whose daughter was about to marry the most powerful prince in the land. Then there was me, the sack of potatoes in a saddle, and Carmelina bringing up the rear. Her horse was wandering lazily under a slack rein. The princess gazed out at the heat-shimmered olive groves, day-dreaming no doubt.

'Do hurry up, Carmelina,' I called over my shoulder. Under my breath I added, 'Let's get this over with.'

Carmelina clicked her tongue and trotted up beside me. 'What's gotten into you, Zeraphina?'

'What? What do you mean by that?'

'You're very cranky today. What's wrong?'

'The heat,' I said. The heat was becoming my excuse for everything.

She sighed, eyes on the clear blue sky. 'It's such a beautiful day.'

I pinched the bridge of my nose, certain I had a headache coming on. 'I really wish people would stop saying that.'

Carmelina laughed. 'You *are* in a sulk. Here, have a crystallised strawberry.'

'No. Thank you.' There was nothing more annoying, I decided, than a girl your own age treating you like a child and offering you sweeties.

There were many riders and wagons on the road into town and we proceeded slowly, but not by design. Passers-by stopped to rubberneck at the bride-to-be and the foreign queen. As we descended into the market square, I groaned. It was packed, barely room to walk, let alone ride a horse through. We tethered our mounts at a nearby tea shop.

'Carmelina,' Renata said. 'Where is the best place to buy fabric? Zeraphina and I will need lots of new dresses in the Pergamian style for when we return to Amentia. We're going to start a trend, aren't we, Daughter?'

'Hmph,' I said.

Renata slapped a coin purse in my hand and hissed, 'Since you left that cat at the palace I was hoping to see you without a puss on today.'

Carmelina danced around me. 'I think she's jealous of Princess Lilith, my Queen. She wishes she was about to marry someone as handsome as my brother.'

The rotten little suck.

We shopped. I gazed, uninterested, at the stalls. It wasn't as exciting as it had looked from my window. There was a lot of junk for sale: cheap trinkets that looked like they'd turn your neck and earlobes green; drums made from badly cured animal skins; wonky pottery. As we progressed the wares improved in quality, but nothing took my fancy. As the others pawed bolts of fabric, I dawdled at a book stall. I could feel one of the guards' eyes on me, nervous that I might wander off, no doubt. There were a lot of tawdry novels and dusty books in strange languages. I picked up a particularly old and worn-out volume titled *Creetchers Moste Fowl*. The title was vaguely amusing. Did it contain monstrous chickens? I thumbed through it, preoccupied by thoughts of Rodden with my ring around his neck. But then I did a double-take. There was a crude sketch of a cloaked creature on one of the pages, and beneath it in curly script were the words 'The Lharmellins'.

My head snapped up. 'How much?' I asked the stall-keeper, waving the book under his nose. I gave him the coins and, as the book was small and I could think of nowhere else to conceal it, I shoved it down the front of my dress.

I hurried back to the others and saw Renata holding up some striped red fabric.

'Lovely, Mother, just what I need. You should get it. All done? I think it's about time we were getting back. We don't want to be late for the banquet tonight.' There was to be yet another dinner in honour of the happy couple. The gorging, it seemed, was to be endless.

'With your colouring? Nonsense, darling.' Renata put the fabric down. 'It's scarcely two hours past midday, and this fabric is revolting. You just browse away and we'll be done in no time.'

I scowled. I knew what 'no time' meant when she was shopping. It meant until the end of time. I pulled Carmelina away from a basket of ribbons. The time for subterfuge was over. 'What's Rodden up to in his turret? He's got all sorts of strange paraphernalia up there. And rabbits as well.'

Carmelina studied my face. 'How do you know what he's got in his room?'

'I went up there, you ninny,' I hissed. 'But that's not the point. It looks like he's doing all sorts of experiments and things. And he stole something from me.' I held my hand aloft. 'My thumb ring.'

Carmelina looked at my hand. 'There *is* a ring on your thumb.'

'My other ring, silly. I had two.' I knew I shouldn't be saying any of this to Carmelina. At best, she'd think I was mad. At worst, she would tell her father and then I'd be for it.

'What would Rodden want with your ring?'

'I don't know. But he threatened me.'

'When did he threaten you?'

'When he found me in his room.'

Carmelina clasped her hands over her mouth in horror. 'Are you stark staring mad?' she asked. 'Couldn't you have been more careful?'

'I was careful,' I hissed. 'I hid under the bed.'

'And how did that work out for you?'

'Oh, shut up. He's up to something,' I said. 'And I don't like it. He's . . .' And I knew I shouldn't say anything, but I couldn't help myself. 'He's a spy,' I blurted.

Carmelina looked at me like I was nuttier than nougat.

I grabbed her arm. 'You need to tell me what it is he does all day. I know he's up to something.'

'Zeraphina, I think your brain is melting in the heat. You need to stop thinking about Rodden.'

'What's that supposed to mean?'

'I mean I think you've got a bit of a thing for him and it's making you crazy.' She patted my hand. 'I've seen this before. He has that effect on girls who've been shut up in gloomy old castles all their lives and have nothing to look forward to but a paunchy, balding husband. You wouldn't be the first to try to elope with him. But really, Zeraphina, he's not interested.'

I took my hand from her matronly grasp. 'I'll be with the horses when you're all done,' I muttered. I stomped off into the crowd, furious with everyone, including myself. I shouldn't have opened my big, fat mouth.

Down the front of my dress the book was getting all sweaty and uncomfortable, but I left it there. I didn't want Renata or Rodden or somebody else taking it away from me before I could read it.

———

As soon as I was alone in my room I tore the book out and flicked to the page I had seen at the bookstall. I studied the sketch. The Lharmellin looked horrid; long and thin and cloaked in black, floating just above the rocky ground. Black trees grew around it. A lipless mouth bared dozens of thin, pointy teeth in a grotesque grimace. Light blazed from its eyes, eyes that seemed to have neither pupils nor irises, made huge by sunken cheeks. The thing was looking straight out of the page, and I couldn't get over the impression that it was looking right at me. Its withered fingers were outstretched and it seemed to be reaching for me with its clawed hands. In the background was a craggy mountain range, desolate and treeless. It looked just like the place in my vision.

Carmelina had been right that day in the gardens: Lharmellins were not human. To think that a creature such as this existed just across the Straits of Unctium made me shiver. It was a relief that they looked so decidedly un-human. So what was I? The question burned in my mind.

I read the accompanying passage:

The moste Terrifying and Rottenn Speecies in all the land, this Lowely Creetcher hides in the tors of Lharmell, feasting on Blud from the Humans it kidnaps. Some they turn into Harmings, who are then maid to join there Sordid Ranks. The Lharmellins are impervious to Human weapons, and have only been thus far Contained to the tors by the Warm Climate surrounding Lharmell, as they are Reluctant to venture out of the colde.

I dropped the book in horror. Harmings? Human Lharmellins? I looked again at the picture. The Lharmellin had light blazing from its eyes, just like Rodden, the blue-eyed phantom, had. The sketch was in black and white, but I felt sure that if the artist had used colour, the light would be ice-blue.

Made to join their sordid ranks.

His eyes. The secrets. The strange goings-on in his room. Rodden was a harming? But did that mean I was, too?

Renata came in and I stuffed the book under a cushion. She held out a gown. 'This one tonight, I think.'

I groaned. 'Please. Not tonight. I'm too tired. I don't feel well. I think I've got sunstroke.'

She placed a cool hand against my brow. 'You don't seem tired, you haven't got a fever and you're not burnt. Get dressed.'

The last thing I wanted to do was to act normal when I was worried there was a horrible lipless monster lurking inside me. I stomped around as I got ready, letting Renata know that I was seriously displeased. But stomping around on marble wasn't nearly as effective as stomping around on the wooden floors at home, and it sent such terrible shocks up my legs, so I stopped.

While we walked to the great hall I pulled Lilith a few paces back. 'Have you noticed anything strange going on?' I whispered to her.

She looked at me in surprise. 'Like what?'

'Like with this war.'

'Oh, Lothskorn's got that under control,' she said breezily.

'Yes, but for whom?'

'What do you mean?'

I searched her face. Her surprise was genuine. Either I was going mad or she was impervious to everything inside her wedding-bubble.

'Oh, nothing,' I muttered, and let go of her arm. I wasn't going to make the same mistake twice: Carmelina already thought I was crazy. I didn't want my own sister thinking the same thing.

To my chagrin, I had to sit next to Rodden again. He appeared at my side as soon as I entered the hall and offered his arm.

'I thought you'd like to keep an eye on me,' he murmured in my ear, as if we were conspirators. He smiled down at me, a mocking, unpleasant smile. Everyone was watching so I had to take his arm, though touching him made me shudder.

'Are you cold, my dear?' Rodden asked, all politeness.

'Don't talk to me, don't look at me, and don't touch me,' I said, taking my arm back as soon as we reached the high table.

He snorted. 'That's rich, coming from someone I found only yesterday hiding under my bed. It's me who should be warning you off.'

I took a sip of water and looked in the other direction.

'Your Majesty.' Rodden's voice rang out. The whole court turned to look at him, including me. He was standing and looking at the king, a smile on his face and a devilish twinkle in his eye. I saw a few young women seated just below us nudge each other and whisper behind their hands.

'Your Majesty,' he said. 'I am aware that preparations for the wedding of the prince and princess are going splendidly. As the happy occasion is still a few days off, I propose a small diversion.' He glanced down at me, his grin wolfish.

Uh-oh.

'Just the other day, Princess Zeraphina was boasting to me of her prowess with a bow. As you know, I like to dabble in the sport.'

The off-hand way he said it made me certain that 'dabble' was a gross understatement.

'I would like to challenge Zeraphina to an archery tournament, winner takes all.'

Everyone turned to look at me in wonderment. The girls who had been admiring Rodden started to titter.

'What a splendid idea!' King Askar cried. Below us, the room broke out into approving applause.

'If she wins, I promise to grant Zeraphina anything that it is in my power to give.' Rodden turned to me, fingering the silver chain at his throat. 'Do you agree, Zeraphina?' he prompted.

I looked up at him, my eyes narrowed. Amusement was etched on his features. I did want my ring back, and King Askar was looking at me expectantly. I reasoned that if I refused it would disappoint the king, and Renata wouldn't want me to do that. She was going to be upset enough about my boasting. Not that I *had* been boasting – not verbally anyway – but she wasn't going to believe me now. Really, accepting the challenge would be the lesser of two evils. Also, I would definitely beat Rodden and nothing would give me more satisfaction. 'I agree, Your Majesty,' I said, inclining my head.

'And if I win,' Rodden continued, grinning out at the court below us, 'I claim Zeraphina's hand in marriage.'

I started to say, 'Now, hang on –' but the entire court erupted into cheers, wolf-whistles and table-banging and I was drowned out. I looked to the king, expecting him to interject on my behalf, but he was applauding and saying 'Splendid! Splendid!'

How could he condone his soon-to-be daughter-in-law's sister marrying a commoner? Where was his sense of propriety? I was a princess!

Now that he was confident of the support of the king, Rodden toasted the room with his wine goblet, looking as if he'd already won the tournament. There was no way I could back out now so I flashed a smile at the court. This brought on even more cheers. Renata glared down the table at me, but really, she was the least of my worries. Why, oh why had I agreed without hearing all the terms? He'd tricked me, making me think all that was at stake was my ring.

Rodden took his seat as soon as the cheers died down. I clenched my hands in my lap, not trusting myself to reach for anything in case I slapped him, right there in front of everyone. I tried to keep the smile in place, but my fury must have shown.

'Starting to doubt your talents?'

'Not in the least,' I spat.

'Now, now, Zeraphina. Don't be like that. Aren't you secretly hoping you'll lose? Carmelina told me about your little crush.'

My face flamed red. Oh, she hadn't! I looked down the table at her. She grinned back at me – she had told. It was too much. Not only had he got the upper hand, he thought I *liked* him.

He leaned closer, dropping his voice. 'You know what makes this all the more sweet? Your ring. I don't even need it any more.'

I stared at him, uncomprehending.

'You're here in Pergamia, aren't you?' His blue eyes were dancing with amusement.

'You've got the whole court in the palm of your hand. But you don't fool me.' I didn't bother to mask the pure hatred on my face. 'And you'll never have me, either. I'll die first.'

As I fled the dais I heard Rodden say to the king, 'Nerves, Your Majesty, nerves.'

———

It wasn't long before Renata appeared, with Lilith just behind her. I was curled up on the sofa, a cushion clutched to my belly. I hadn't been faking to get away from Rodden. I really did feel ill, as if I'd swallowed a dozen angry snakes and they were all writhing around in my belly. Renata stood in front of me without saying anything. Her foot was tapping on the marble floor so I knew she was just warming herself up. Choosing the right words to blast me with. Lilith hung in the doorway, keeping away from the storm that was about to break but curious just same. I'd be curious too if I was about to see my sister flayed alive.

Renata opened her mouth, and then closed it again. Then she opened it.

Here it came. The word-barrage.

But she just threw up her hands and stalked out.

'Aren't you going to bawl me out?' I called.

She strode back. Perhaps I should have kept my mouth shut.

'You,' she said, pointing a finger at me, 'had better hope that you're as good an archer as you say you are, or that he is a terrible one. Because if you lose, there's nothing I will be able to do to prevent this marriage. What leverage do I have? They take words of honour very seriously in Pergamia, and with Lilith on the brink of her own marriage to the king's son I can hardly go around making demands. It could jeopardise everything.' Her eyes narrowed. 'Unless you want to lose. This isn't some plan the two of you have hatched up? You haven't fallen in love with him, have you?' Renata said 'love' as if it was the most despicable thing in the world. Then again, loving Rodden would be rather despicable.

'No! Oh, yuck, love Rodden? You've got to be kidding. He's an absolute creep.'

'Really?' Lilith piped up. 'Amis says he's the best person in the world.'

'Amis needs to get out more.'

'And he said –' Lilith stopped.

Renata turned to her eldest. 'And he said *what*?'

Lilith looked apologetic and twisted her hands this way and that. 'And he said . . . he's a really good shot.'

Renata covered her eyes with her hands and groaned. I did the same with the cushion.

'Oh, look on the bright side, Zeraphina,' Lilith said.

I looked up from behind the cushion. There was a bright side?

'After you've married him, we'll be able to see each other every day.'

'No you won't, because I will have thrown myself off the battlements on the morning of my wedding.'

'Don't be so dramatic, you silly girl. What you are going to do is get yourself down the archery range first thing in the morning and practise, practise, practise. No daughter of mine is going to marry some trumped-up politician because of a ridiculous bet. We'll be the laughing stock of all Brivora.'

I pressed my face into the cushion again.

'I don't think you're helping, Mother,' I heard Lilith whisper. She must have steered Renata out of the room, because when I came up for air Lilith was sitting beside me and Renata was nowhere in sight. Then, in the silence, I could hear her muttering from the next room.

I rolled my eyes. 'Thanks.'

Lilith shrugged. 'She's overreacting. I know you're a good shot. Anyway . . .'

'Anyway what?'

'If you do lose . . .'

'Don't even say it!'

'Oh, Fina, come on. I know you like him. You're always looking at him.'

'That's because he's up to something.'

'Don't be so childish. He's very handsome and you have a crush. Just admit it. And he's a good person. He's devoted his life to the protection of Pergamia. He's fiercely protective of Amis, too. Do you know Amis would have turned me down if Rodden hadn't approved of me?'

I wanted to tell her that it was because Amis, and everyone else in Pergamia, was blind to the truth. Everyone except me. I was going to prove he was a monster. But first, I had to make sure that I didn't end up as his wife.

EIGHT

When I went down to the practice range the next morning at Renata's insistence, Rodden was there. Not firing, just standing around. Waiting for me. When he saw me he grinned and leaned against the wall, arms folded. I ignored him, notching up a few arrows and firing them, but I could feel his eyes on me. It put me off and my shots were way off target. Every misfired arrow brought a snort of amusement from him.

'Don't you have anything better to do?' I asked, not taking my eyes off the bullseye. I would hit it this time. I would.

'What could be more pleasant than watching you make a fool of yourself? Unlike you, I'm sure of my skill. I don't need to practise.'

My fingers were slippery with nervous sweat and the arrow loosed before I had finished drawing back. It fired sluggishly and rebounded off the board.

He laughed. 'Don't worry, sweetheart. Whichever way it goes you'll still get a ring.' He waggled the third finger of his left hand at me.

I unstrung my bow with a snap. Stuff practice. I wasn't going to stand around being tormented all day. I stomped past him and made my way to the stables. I needed to get away; far, far away. Besides, if I went back to my room Renata would give me hell about not practising. She wouldn't understand that if I wasn't ready now, I never would be.

I asked a groom to saddle up a horse for me – with a proper saddle, not one of those silly side-saddles. I want to gallop.

Reasoning that it looked like the only semi-deserted place near the palace, I headed for the forest to the north-west, outside the heavily guarded walls. I wanted to get out of sight of Rodden and all his soldier minions. Away from the northern turret.

The horse was shiny brown like a chestnut and was eager to get some exercise. We raced up a narrow track through the trees and I was exceedingly glad to leave Rodden, Renata and the whole palace behind me. Tree branches grew low across the track and I flattened myself against the horse's neck so I wouldn't be swiped off. The wind sent my hair flying like streamers.

Sooner than I would have liked, the forest thinned and we could go no further. We'd reached the edge of a cliff and beyond it was the sea. I dismounted, walked to the edge and looked down. It was a sheer drop. Waves crashed against half-submerged rocks.

My thoughts grew morbid. Here was where I would throw myself off if I lost the tournament tomorrow. It would make a good bards' tale.

Hear me now, hear me now. I am Yorris the Bard, who heard this tale from Derko the Bard, who heard it from Heppo the Bard, and all the bards before him. Gather to me, and hear the tale of the beautiful, clever princess whom no one would listen to but was right all along about the evil, depraved monster who had all great Brivora in his thrall . . .

It would end with Renata weeping over my dead and pallid body as it lay on the beach, attractively scattered with seaweed. What a shame I wouldn't be alive to hear it sung. The last part sounded especially sweet.

If I lost. But I wasn't going to. I'd been practising since I was eight.

I shaded my eyes and peered across the ocean. I almost expected to see dark and forbidding mountains, the tors of Lharmell, rising in the distance. But all I saw was a gleaming horizon.

To the west was the city dock, cluttered with sailing and fishing ships. From this distance they looked as tiny as toys. There were several more on the open water, their sails filled with wind as they ripped along. The freedom they commanded was intoxicating; the whole wide blue yonder was theirs.

To the east stretched a curving, sandy expanse of coast. Waves crashed against an empty beach, sending plumes of spray up into the air.

So this was the sea. Living as I did in a land-locked, mountainous country I had never imagined that it would be so big, so blue and so noisy. Holding the horse by its bridle, I made my way along the cliff until I found a path down to the beach. I took off my boots and tied my practice dress around my thighs. Over the wind and crashing waves I could hear the screaming cries of the white and grey gulls that wheeled overhead. They coasted the strong wind, moving neither forwards nor backwards. Foamy water rushed in and covered my ankles before rushing out again. Despite my glum mood, the shock of cold water made me squeal and hop about. As the wave receded it stole grains of sand from beneath my feet. It was one of the oddest sensations I had ever felt, the earth being pulled from under me.

Things didn't stay the same; I was starting to understand that. In a few days Lilith would be married and gone forever. Of course, she wouldn't be *gone*, but she would never be just my big sister again, the one who had the bedroom down the hall and all the time in the world to lie around with me on rainy days. She would be Princess of Pergamia, and one day, Queen Lilith. I imagined what it would feel like, going home without her, and I felt a squeeze in my throat. I didn't want things to change. They were changing faster than they ever had in my life and showed no sign of slowing down. This time next year I could be married. This time tomorrow I could be betrothed if I didn't win the tournament.

I looked out to the north, the direction of the greatest uncertainty of all. On such a bright day it was difficult to imagine that, just out of my sight, was a cold, mountainous country filled with malevolent beings. And that just behind me, barely a mile off, Rodden Lothskorn sat in his turret plotting who knew what. The man was an enigma. Why tell me to go home one moment and then construct an elaborate plan to force me into marriage the next? It didn't make any sense.

Unless it was to discredit me before the court. If he won and I refused him, everyone would know I'd gone back on my word, however unwittingly it had been given in the first place. No one would believe me after that if I accused him of spying for the enemy.

Or – and this was an even more startling thought – he intended to marry me in order to hand me over to the Lharmellins.

Whatever the reason, it didn't originate from any affectionate feelings, I was certain.

The sun was biting into my bare shoulders so I waded out of the water and mounted my horse. I let it set its own pace as we headed for the castle. I was in no hurry to get back.

I had not gone fifty feet when a gnawing pain clawed at my back. I gasped and straightened, trying to work out what I imagined to be a knot. The pain grew worse, and five minutes later I was sweating profusely. Shaking, I slid from the horse's back and pressed my face against its flank. The pain dimmed as I stood there, but when I started forward, it erupted again with greater violence. It felt like a thousand claws had dug into the flesh of my back.

If I stepped backwards, there was no pain; forwards, and the agony began.

I was no great judge of direction, but the coastline told me that behind lay true north, the direction of Lharmell.

With tears springing into my eyes, I again mounted my horse. Burying my face in its sweet-smelling mane, I urged it onwards, south towards the palace.

My shrieks of pain ricocheted around the bare trunks of the forest, only falling silent in the blessed moments when I lost consciousness.

———

Renata looked up from the sofa as soon as I entered our apartment.

'Did you practise?' she asked.

'Yes,' I said, going straight through to my room before she could see my white face and shaking hands. It had taken hours to make the return journey, whereas outward it had been merely minutes. Somewhere close to the castle walls the pain had dimmed. I had leaned gratefully against the cool, white walls for several minutes and composed my streaky face and sweat-soaked figure.

As far as Renata knew, I had practised for many hours.

———

Despite the wedding of his only son being just days away, King Askar pulled out all the stops for the tournament. In a grassy field within the palace grounds a temporary range had been set up. Two dozen targets were at one end of the field. There were to be more contestants than just Rodden and me, I found out. A royal decree had been issued the very evening of the challenge, inviting all archers within fifty miles to enter the competition. Amis told me this when I had come down to the field and found it full of people stringing bows.

'They're not *all* being offered my hand in marriage, are they?'

'No,' he assured me. 'If somebody else wins, they get a coin prize. But no one else is going to win.'

'You mean you think Rodden's going to win.'

'I don't know,' he said, giving me a sidelong glance. 'Lilith's been telling me just how good her little sister is. This should be interesting.' He grinned.

Interesting. Yes, like a trip to the tooth-surgeon.

Lilith gave me a kiss and a hasty 'Good luck!' before Amis took her hand and they went to their places in the royal marquee. Multi-coloured tents had been erected around the field, a-flutter with little flags. Spectators from the city were filing in through the front gates. They sat on the rows and rows of benches that had been carried down from the great hall. Stalls were selling cups of pink lemonade and honey biscuits. Children ran all over the gardens with toy bows and rubber-tipped arrows. A group of girls in party dresses threw a red ball between them. A coconut shy had been set up. The atmosphere was that of a carnival. The whole of Xallentaria was treating this event as little more than a diversion.

Everywhere I went, people pointed at me and gawked openly. I overheard snippets of their conversations: I was the proud princess from the south who'd bitten off more than she could chew; Rodden was their champion, the kingdom's saviour. He was tipped to win and take this arrogant foreigner down a peg or two, and then marry her to boot. He was the darling of the masses, a man who could show them that no matter how low-born you were, you could still end up gentry by a twist of fate. I, on the other hand, represented the misplaced pride of a spoilt royal. I would have found their ignorance amusing if I wasn't so nervous about my own fate.

Bets were being placed and the odds were fifty-to-one in Rodden's favour. No one thought I was going to win.

I stood outside my warm-up tent, Leap at my feet and Griffin perched on the back of a chair. They watched the proceedings with interest; a bow in my hands usually meant quiet, solitude, a chance to hunt; but they seemed to be enjoying the crowd. I rolled my sleeves up past my elbows so I didn't get too hot and took my gauntlet off, buckling my arm guards on in its place. All I could do now was wait. I glanced towards the royal tent. The king and queen sat on their thrones, laughing and talking to a few lords and ladies, and supping from silver goblets and little platters. Amis and Lilith were engrossed with each other, talking intently and holding hands. Rodden stood confidently nearby, chatting with a baron's daughter or two and leaning casually on his bow, clearly at ease. The girls pulled ribbons from their hair and knelt down to tie them to the butt of his bow for luck. More girls saw this and went over to him, and soon there was a rainbow of ribbons fluttering from his bow. One girl leaned in to kiss his cheek.

The people's favourite, I thought with scorn.

Renata sat next to the queen, the only one apart from me not enjoying the festivities. She must have heard what people were saying. Either that or she was still livid that I had gotten myself into this mess. But when I caught her eye she gave me a small smile and jutted her jaw: *chin up, Zeraphina*. Family pride to the last. I was glad for her support, but she must have heard that pride always comes before a fall.

Rodden and I were the last event of the day. First would be the children's contest; the ladies'; the soldiers', which would give the king an opportunity to exhibit his army's prowess; several opens; and then, finally, the main event: Rodden and I and the winners from the opens.

For the children's round, the targets were set at ten paces. Boys and girls lined up, mostly soldiers' children. More than a few gangly girls had entered, and they cast shy smiles at me. It seemed I was popular with one group at least.

I was too keyed up to pay close attention to the heats. Row after row of archers lined up, and as the events progressed the targets moved further and further away. The soldiers drew the most cheers as they took the opportunity to show off with some fancy shots. One drew a circle of arrows around the rim of the target. A group of nine lined up and fired at once, their arrows spelling out a capital 'A' in honour of the king. To them, it was more of a display than a competition. Hoggit was there and he was particularly vocal, calling out to the crowd and strutting around between shots. I had to admit that as a group they were quite proficient. But I was better.

It was the opens that I paid close attention to. Among their ranks might be a maverick, a lone-wolf archer who was going to steal the day; someone better even than Rodden and me. I prayed for such a thing. If neither Rodden nor I won, all bets would be off: I wouldn't get my ring back and he wouldn't get my hand. This, I decided, was the second-best outcome. I didn't need to get my ring back from Rodden. As he'd said, it was useless to him now. I was already here.

None of this was going to change my game-plan, however. If I slackened off to allow someone else to win and Rodden beat them, I would be lost. I was going to compete to the best of my ability and just hope that if I wasn't as good as Rodden, another would be better than both of us.

Someone in the last open caught my attention. It was a tall man, cloaked in black. Without emotion, he fired shot after perfect shot and ended up winning the heat. Rodden noticed him too, consternation on his features. I saw him lean across to say something in Amis's ear. The prince frowned and looked at the man, and then called Hoggit over. The captain listened, nodded, and went back to his archers. There were already a handful of guards on the field, but those who had competed suddenly snapped to attention and posted themselves around the range as well, their eyes on the cloaked figure.

What was Rodden up to? Was this stranger too good, and he was going to stoop to murder rather than lose the tournament? But surely if this was the plan he wouldn't have involved the prince. I studied Rodden's face, but instead of fierce competitiveness, I saw unease. I looked back at the stranger but couldn't detect anything dangerous about him. Besides, he was one man against a hundred, so what could happen?

I didn't have much time to consider this as the final event was being called. Stomach lurching, I stepped forward. As the main attraction, Rodden and I were given pride of place at the centre of the range. The other contestants fell in beside us. The man in the black cloak took his place next to Rodden. I saw Rodden's shoulders bunch, and a ripple of distaste go through him. Good. He was worried. As my rival's confidence waned, I found mine grew, and I plucked at my string in a cheerful manner. Renata and Lilith were on their feet, the only ones cheering for me. Two sharp-eyed girls aged around eighteen or so had made it to the final round. They looked like soldiers' daughters and were long-legged and tanned. One of them must have been Hoggit's as he hollered and applauded like crazy when she took her place. Two soldiers and one other civilian took their marks.

The rules were simple: six sets of three arrows were to be fired, and at the end of the round all but the top three archers were to be eliminated. The remaining three would go through to the final round. Before any shots had been fired I was certain that the final round would consist of Rodden, me, and the stranger in black. The judges cautioned the audience to remain silent throughout to allow the competitors complete concentration.

The targets were set at fifty paces, which gave those with heavier bows like myself and the men an advantage. Smaller bows would not fire with enough force to be unaffected by the cross-wind that had started blowing.

Lilith stepped forward to start the tournament. I could see from her face that she thought the whole affair was amusing. She held aloft a fluttering hanky which she released with the words, 'Let the tournament begin!'

We took our marks, notched our arrows, drew back and, as one, fired. Arrows whistled through the air and hit the targets with a dull *thunk*. A murmur went through the crowd. I let out the breath I'd been holding: from my target sprouted a perfect bullseye. I had told myself that I wouldn't look at anyone's board but my own, but despite myself I snuck a glance at Rodden's and the stranger's. Theirs showed perfects shots as well.

Despite the butterflies in my stomach, I steeled myself to focus. We fired shot after shot and soon I was in my stride. Notch, draw, aim, fire. After each set of three, squires ran forward to clear our boards. The stranger's arrows were embedded so deeply that the boy had to brace himself with his foot in order to yank them out.

At the end of the round the scorers totted up the points. The contestants shuffled from foot to foot. I bit my thumbnail. The stranger stared straight ahead, motionless.

The announcer called the names of those eliminated. As I had predicted, the last ones standing were the stranger, Rodden and myself.

Rodden turned to me and bowed. 'Congratulations, Your Highness.' To the crowd he looked gracious, but I could see the sardonic glint in his eyes. As he congratulated me he pulled my ring out from beneath his shirt where I could see it. Odious man.

The final round consisted of sets of two shots. At the end of each set a competitor could be eliminated. If no one slipped, the sets would continue until someone misfired from fatigue. The crowd was spellbound; the only noise was the wind. We had all fired equally well so far, so no one was sure which way it was going to go.

I forced myself to concentrate. I imagined that I was in Amentia and a long, chilly afternoon of perfect shots stretched before me. As if to lend authenticity to this, Leap padded to my side and sat blinking in the sun. My mascot caught the crowd's attention and they oohed and ahhed over him.

We drew back; fired. And again: draw; fire. The wind was blowing harder, gusting erratically. I began to be careful when I loosed my shots; a stray gust could blow an arrow off course. I waited until a particularly vicious wind had just begun to subside and fired before a fresh one could get up to speed. The others noticed my technique and adjusted their shots as well.

After four sets Rodden and I were still as steady as rocks, but the stranger had begun to wheeze. Fatigue was getting to him. For the first time I noticed his hands. They were gnarled and withered and a grim shade of grey. Puffy blue veins stood out over his tendons.

On the second shot of the sixth set the stranger misfired. The crowd let out a collective gasp. Holding my breath, I looked to the scorers as they deliberated. At last one looked away from the board and drew his arm in a sharp, horizontal line: the stranger was out.

I let out my breath, but in dismay rather than relief: the hardest part was yet to come. Neither Rodden nor I had shown signs of tiring. I had a feeling that many more sets stretched before us.

The scorers moved our targets back five paces, upping the stakes.

By the sixteenth set, the first two fingers of my left hand were red raw. By the twenty-first, my shoulders were beginning to cramp. The gusts were blowing harder and more haphazardly. It was getting more difficult to correct for the wind and predict when it was safe to fire.

I loosed the second arrow of the twenty-second set and my hopes plummeted. Before the arrow even sank into the board I knew it had been blown off course. I'd fired too soon. It was inside the bullseye but it was off-centre. Rodden's arrow bit into his board a split-second later. Feeling like everything was moving in slow motion, I turned to look at his target. He'd caught the tail-end of the gust; he'd fired too soon as well, as he'd been taking his cue from me. I looked from his arrow to mine, hoping to see a difference, but I couldn't. The murmur from the crowd became a rumble as the scorers stepped forward with measuring tapes, trying to discern any difference in the shots that the naked eye couldn't perceive.

I knew it was down to this. One of us had been unluckier with that wind. The scorers deliberated in whispers, measuring and remeasuring. Finally, one of them tapped Rodden's board and drew his arm in a sharp, horizontal line: Rodden was out.

The crowd erupted wildly. Renata and Lilith were jumping up and down.

I had won.

Rodden turned to me, a wry smile on his face. He took my hand, bowed, and kissed it. Then he turned to face the crowd and held up my arm, signifying my victory. Everyone cheered and stamped their feet. Their favourite had lost, but he was still heroic in their eyes, taking his defeat with grace and good humour.

Rodden walked off, unfastening his arm guards as he went, but the crowd was still cheering and I realised the cheers were for me, not him. The underdog had snatched victory in the face of extreme odds and they loved it.

Despite the tears of relief that were accumulating behind my eyelids, I smiled and waved to the crowd. It was over. I wasn't going to marry Rodden. Before anyone could come over and congratulate me I ran from the range and hid behind a tent, needing a moment to collect myself. Angrily, I rubbed my eyes with the heels of my hands, trying to grind out the tears.

When I looked up my vision was blurred and there was a black shape standing in front of me. As I was furiously blinking to clear my eyes, it reached for me. It was the stranger in black. I felt a jolt of fear: we were out of sight of the archers and something about the cloaked figure screamed danger. I wanted to run but my feet were rooted to the spot. I felt the hand close over my wrist –

From behind, someone grabbed a fistful of my dress and yanked me backwards.

'Hey!' My vision finally cleared and I saw Rodden, holding me behind him, a hand pressed against my shoulder. He leaned forward and said something to the man that I couldn't make out. The figure looked from Rodden to me, as if weighing up the situation. Then he turned and left.

Rodden turned and shook my shoulder angrily, his eyes blazing. 'Be more careful, will you?'

'What? I was just standing here.' But he was already stalking away.

Now I really did want to cry. Nothing was making any sense. I felt none of the happiness I should have for winning the tournament. Rodden was still acting like he was in charge. I didn't feel like a winner. I felt like a stupid child.

I drew in a ragged breath. Spots danced before my eyes and I staggered. I was suddenly breathless. I doubled over, the hunger blooming in my chest and rippling like wildfire down my limbs. *No, not here.* There was nowhere to hide.

'Zeraphina!' The cry seemed to come from a long way off. It sounded like Renata. I didn't want her to see me like this so I tried to run. My legs gave out and I dropped to the ground. I curled my body around the pain. It could be fatigue, the sleepless nights and strain of the tournament overcoming me. But I was fooling myself. It was the hunger. I heard a roaring in my ears, felt hands on me, then nothing.

NINE

I opened my eyes to utter blackness. I sat up, flailing around, and immediately got tangled in netting. I panicked, claustrophobia setting in. Why was it so dark? It was like the dungeon in my dream. *The darkness. The blood. Lilith's dead body.* I fought my way out of the bed and felt for the balcony door. It had been closed and the curtains were drawn across it, but my frantic fingers soon located the handle and I flung myself outside. I discovered the reason for the darkness: it was night. I had slept the day away. I felt groggy and weak and slumped onto a bench.

Through my fogginess, a sound on the wind came to me, softly at first, but then it pierced through my sleep-haze. It was the eerie, wordless chanting, louder than ever. The sound filled my ears and I searched the sky.

The moon was waxing full. A dark shape passed over it and I thought I saw the flap of wings. It was either small and very close, or huge and far away. My impression was the latter. I couldn't see much of the sky from there so I ran out of the apartment and along the deserted passages.

I found the stairs to the parapet and flew up them. I was dimly aware of Leap and Griffin at my side. We went up and up in the darkness, my hands clawing at the walls in my desperation to reach the top. I burst out into the night and searched the sky. In the dim moonlight I saw shapes moving overhead, blotting out the stars. There must have been hundreds of them. I ran to the edge of the parapet, straining to see what they were.

A voice spoke over the keening wind. 'Feeling better?'

In my haste I hadn't seen that Rodden was standing on the parapet. The sky began to clear.

'Where are they going?' I wailed. As the stars reappeared I felt a terrible sense of loss.

'Where do you think?'

I watched as the shapes receded. To the north. Where else? I slumped against the battlements. 'No,' I whispered.

'No what?'

'No, I'm not feeling better. I feel worse. What were those things? Lharmellins?'

He didn't answer me.

'Did you make the singing stop?' I asked.

He turned to leave, but I grabbed his arm. 'Not so fast.' I held out my hand. 'My ring.'

He dug into his pocket and slapped it onto my palm without a word. Then he pulled out of my grasp and made for his turret.

'No! Please. Talk to me. I need to know what's going on.'

He rounded on me. 'You really have no idea? I'm amazed. You do enough snooping around.'

'I think I know what I am. I think I know what you are. But I don't know what you and *they* are up to, and it's driving me crazy. And that thing today in the cloak. What was he? And what was in the sky just now?'

I saw relief on his face. He was glad of my ignorance, which meant he wasn't going to tell me anything. I turned to go, but it was his turn to call me back.

'Zeraphina, wait.'

I waited for him to speak, but he didn't. Instead, he held out his wrist and Griffin flew from the battlements and landed carefully on his sleeve. He hadn't whistled or even looked at her. Then Leap jumped onto the ledge and butted his head against Rodden's shoulder. I felt a huge pang of loss. They were deserting me. My only friends were being taken from me.

'How did you do that?' I whispered. For the second time that day I was close to tears. 'Griffin doesn't go to anyone but me.'

'I asked her to,' he said.

He wasn't making sense. He hadn't said a word. 'No you didn't.'

'Not with my voice. I spoke in my head. They can hear me. They can hear *you*. Haven't you ever realised?'

I shook my head. Hear me?

Zeraphina . . .

I felt a jolt. It was the voice in my not-dream. The voice of the blue-eyed phantom, the one that had soothed the burning hunger from my body and driven away the keening wind. I knew that voice better than anything in the world. I heard it in my dreams. 'You try it,' he said.

Tentatively, I held out my wrist and called to Griffin, speaking her name with my mind. Nothing happened. I tried Leap, begging for him to come to me. He didn't move.

'I can't –' My voice caught. I stepped forward and clutched Leap to my body, burying my face in his familiar fur. Why was Rodden so cruel? I didn't understand any of this.

He sighed. 'I forgot. I made them give you laudanum for the hunger. It's made you foggy.'

I shivered in my nightclothes.

'You should go back to bed,' he said, and walked away.

Angry, I whistled for Griffin and she came, a flash of gold over my head. I trudged to my room, angry that he'd given me still more questions instead of answers. I hugged Leap to my chest and kept my eyes on my eagle, her wingtips brushing the walls as she flew.

―――

'Here.' Renata handed me a tall glass of water. I sipped cautiously, still feeling the woozy effects of the drug I had been given. I was in our rooms on the sofa, my legs curled under me and a blanket around my shoulders. It was nearly midday but I'd only just woken from a fitful sleep. The glass felt too heavy in my hand. My shoulders ached from the strain of the archery tournament and my mind was leaden.

It was mostly from the laudanum, but there was something else. I was fed up. Fed up with not having any answers. Fed up with being kept in the dark. I was also exhausted from the blood-hunger. I remembered what Lilith whispered to me that morning in her room, devastated by Lester's death. *I just want everything to stop. I try to look ahead and it's like there's nothing there.* That was how I felt. I was trapped in Pergamia. I knew that when the time came I would be unable to get in the coach to go home. The Lharmellins had me in their grip. If one of those things had come down from the sky I would have begged for it to take me to the north, even though I was terrified of what it would mean.

So, there it was. I was trapped. In limbo.

Renata reached for my hand but I pulled away. She sat down next to me. 'Lothskorn wants me to take you home,' she said softly.

I started. *Rodden.* My mind was suddenly crisp with rage. 'Why does everyone do everything he wants them to?' I exploded. 'What's *with* him? Is he king all of a sudden?' I struggled off the sofa and glared at her.

'Darling,' said Renata, her voice pitched as if to soothe a wild animal. 'He's worried about you. *I'm* worried about you.'

Worried! He knew I could no sooner go home than fly to the moon. I hurled the glass to the marble floor. It smashed into smithereens, water and shards splattering all over the ground.

Renata stood up. 'Zeraphina!'

I snatched up a vase and hurled it against the far wall. It hit a painting and exploded, and they both went crashing to the ground. This was good. This was just what I needed. To destroy something; feel it break under the force of my hand.

'What's going on?' Lilith came into the room, surveying the damage.

'Zeraphina is throwing a temper tantrum because she doesn't want to go home.'

'But my wedding's tomorrow.'

'See, Mother?' I said. 'Lilith's wedding is tomorrow. Now, how can I miss that?' I stalked to my room. If I had been properly dressed I would have fled the apartment, but I was still in my night-gown. I slammed the door behind me. Leap's ears were flattened against his skull and he looked at me with haunted eyes. I sat down and pulled him onto my lap.

As my anger dissipated I felt a twinge of shame. Renata and Lilith had no idea what I was going through, but that wasn't their fault. All these years I had worked hard to conceal the truth from them. From myself as well. Practising my archery had been the sporting equivalent of putting my head in the sand.

But now, because of my pig-headedness, it was too late: Lilith would marry Amis tomorrow, and Pergamia would become her home for the rest of her life. I couldn't shake the feeling that I'd condemned her to a life in peril. Whatever circled ominously over the keep on a nightly basis was sure to attack before long. My dreams were more prophetic than I'd thought: if Lilith died, her blood would be on my hands, for I had been the one to coerce her northwards.

My head started to ache and I lay down. I must have fallen asleep again because the next thing I heard was Renata and Lilith coming in from dinner. I crept out, blinking in the candlelight. As my eyes cleared I saw that the mess I'd made had been cleared up.

'Were they very valuable?' I croaked.

Renata handed me a flute of something pale and bubbly. 'Not at all, darling. As soon as I saw them I knew they were barely fit to be hurled across a room. Are you feeling better?'

We sat together on the couch and I curled into her warm body. The dress she wore was of the softest satin. I felt like a child who'd been woken by the grown-ups coming home and I relished the cosseted feeling it gave me. I was still the baby of the family.

'A little,' I said.

Lilith sat before us on the ottoman, her eyes shining. She held up her glass. 'What should we toast?'

'That's easy, Daughter. To you and Amis. To the future.'

'To the future,' we echoed, even though it pained me to say the words. I took a sip of the bubbly stuff and it was pleasant, but very dry. Then I sneezed.

Renata took my glass. 'And that's more than enough for you in the state you're in. It's time you were off to bed.'

'No, please. Just a little longer.' I wanted to stay with them in the soft candlelight and just be quiet together. It was the last time Lilith would belong only to us.

Lilith took another sip. 'Tell us about your wedding, Mother.'

Renata smiled softly and dropped her eyes. I was a tale we'd heard only in snatches over the years, and rarely with any joy. Tonight, it seemed, we were to be indulged. 'By the time I was married,' she began, 'I was already queen. My parents were gone and Amentia was mine. It had declined by then, but I expected us to pull through. Of course, we never did. Things just got worse. At the time I wasn't particularly worried. I was quite enjoying myself and had no intention of marrying; men are so dreadfully bossy. Then I met your father.'

'Love at first sight?' asked Lilith.

'Hardly. He was always taunting me about something. It never even crossed our minds that marriage was on the cards: I was a queen and he was a prince, fourth-born and totally landless. It's just not done, you know.'

'Mother,' I reproached. 'Marrying beneath your station.'

'Quite. So, as neither of us was even thinking of marriage, we became friends. Of sorts. More like sparring partners; we were always fighting about something. And then one day he told me I'd have to marry him because I was in love with him, and I was very angry to find he was right.' She was smiling, lost in the past, a place she hadn't dared to go for a very long time. 'And then we had you, Lilith,' she said softly. 'And then before I knew it I was expecting you.' She grasped my hand, her smile fading. 'And then he was gone. We'd had three years.'

Lilith and I were silent. It had been a mistake to ask her about her wedding. The story, as we'd known, had a tragic ending.

Renata gripped my hand hard. 'And that's why I was so afraid to lose you, Zeraphina, when you grew ill. You and Lilith were all I had left of him. I would have done anything to keep you with me. Anything.'

I was too stunned to speak, but the question echoed through my mind.

Anything? What did you do to me?

Lilith wrapped her arms around her, which is what I should have done. Belatedly I joined them, and for a few minutes we were a sticky mess of tears, satin and rouge.

Renata came to the surface first. 'Look at me, my eldest daughter's wedding tomorrow and I'm crying before the service has started. I've had too much wine.'

'Don't they like to *drink* in Pergamia!' said Lilith.

'Yes,' I agreed. 'Have you seen Amis's aunts? They're always tipsy.'

'Outright drunk, more like it,' Renata said. 'You watch. We'll come back to visit your sister next year to find her passed out cold in some bushes.'

Come back. *Leave*. It was an impossibility. The journey home would kill me for sure.

Renata steered me to my room and tucked me into bed.

'Just you and me now, hey?' she whispered, smoothing the sheets. 'Heaven help us.'

I managed a weak smile before the tears, wine and sheer exhaustion knocked me out.

———

I slept until just before dawn, when I was awakened by shouts and running feet. I leaned over my balcony to try to see what was going on, but the commotion had already passed by. As my eyes adjusted to the morning light I saw more archers than ever posted around the battlements, arrows trained on the sky. They looked particularly alarmed and I got the impression that this time it had been a close call. I ran to the door of our apartment and stood outside, listening. There was another commotion going on somewhere, but far off in the keep. The king and queen were being called for. Then things quieted and I crept back inside.

I stood in the darkened sitting room, ears peeled for the sounds of an attack, and I remembered that this was Lilith's wedding day.

As I was being dressed, possibilities were racing across my mind. I could stop the wedding. Tell Lilith she wouldn't be safe if she stayed in Pergamia. *There are monsters across the straits. I think they attacked this morning. I think I'm one of them . . .*

But it was there that my mind recoiled and I knew I couldn't open my mouth. I told myself that it wasn't only cowardice that kept me silent, but a lack of proof: all I had in the way of material evidence was a tawdry paperback from a market stall.

If only I'd voiced my doubts earlier. But hadn't I tried? Hadn't I been trying to find out the truth ever since I'd got to Pergamia, and been laughed at and paraded in front of crowds for my trouble?

I remembered how pleased I had been with myself the morning I had convinced Lilith to come to Pergamia. As I watched her being dressed, her face aglow with excitement, I wondered what sort of life I had condemned her to.

I had one chance left to ensure her safety, but I would have to rely on the most dangerous man in the kingdom: Rodden. I'd stupidly asked for my ring back, voiding his promise to grant me anything I desired, but I had one more bargaining chip. He wanted me to go home. So I would tell him I could stay and kick up a fuss in Pergamia, or he could give me a big bottle of laudanum so I could knock myself out for the whole journey back to Amentia, and promise never to return – if, and this was a big if, he promised to take care of Lilith. Get her out of the way before things turned nasty. And I had a feeling they were going to.

For the wedding, we three wore gowns in the Amentine style, but in summery Pergamian fabrics. Lilith wore white, I was in pale, rosy pink and Renata's gown was deep magenta. I was finding it hard to breath in my corset, and I could barely keep still long enough for Eugenia to make me up.

Renata checked the hour-candle: it was time. She nodded to Lilith and we fell in behind her. Renata was wearing her crown and I had a delicate garland of roses in my hair. Lilith wore a thin white veil sewn to her silver circlet.

The ceremony was to take place in a rose arbour in the garden. We met Amis in the throne room, Renata presenting her eldest to him formally, as if for the first time. The pair bowed with the requisite stiffness, but I could see smiles hovering at the corners of their mouths.

In the Pergamian royal family, it was the king and queen who performed the marriage ceremony. The son or daughter had to present their betrothed and then swear all the things they would and would not do from this day forth, and generally sum up why their parents should consent to the match.

I was so busy scanning for Rodden's dark hair and brooding features as I walked to my place in front that I barely registered the beauty of the rose arbour. By the time I'd reached the front, curtseyed to the king and queen on their ubiquitous thrones, and moved to one side, I knew he wasn't there. Unable to help myself, I kept glancing over my shoulder at the court seated behind me until Renata gave me a stern look.

I couldn't believe Rodden was missing the wedding of his best friend. I had desperately wanted to talk to him before anyone promised anything to anyone. If I didn't like his response I could still have a fainting fit and halt the proceedings until I came up with another plan. There didn't seem much point in fainting now. I would just have to track him down after the ceremony.

The irony of his absence hadn't escaped me: I'd spent my whole time in Pergamia trying to avoid Rodden, and as soon as I wanted him around, he disappeared.

Then Amis was bringing Lilith up the aisle to

his parents. I looked at them, and my anxieties were soothed enough to watch the ceremony, if not actually listen to the words. The pair knelt before the king and queen, bowing their heads. King Askar began a long speech, something about the might of Pergamia and its great, illustrious history. Then Queen Ulah made an even longer speech about the sanctity of marriage. Amis's aunts had snagged a front row seat and I could hear them hiccupping and blowing loudly into handkerchiefs as they wept. Carmelina, standing at the front with me, was tearing up too.

Nothing really filtered through to me until right at the end. Amis had finished his lengthy promises to Lilith and was telling the king and queen why he wanted to marry her. He was looking at Lilith with an open face and a gaze of pure love.

'. . . met her it was like I already knew her. It was like remembering, not learning; seeing, instead of just looking; and not only hearing, but sensing and knowing and feeling all at once. Because we are the same, deep down. And nothing can change that.'

The words were meant to be words of joy, but they stung me. I realised then that no one was ever going to stand up in front of a room full of people and say such things to me. I couldn't let anyone see me how I really was, because I was a monster. I would never find that one person who, deep down, was the same as me. I felt tears start, and I was angry with myself for crying, for feeling sorry for myself. But then Lilith and Amis were standing, facing us all, and everyone was crying, so I let the tears fall over the smile that I made myself wear, for them, because they were in love. And I felt that part of me that was happy for them and I cherished it. Because that part was human, and it was the part that I fervently hoped was the real me.

TEN

Finally, at the wedding feast, he was there. We were celebrating outdoors in the sunshine and I spotted him making his way over the grounds to the banquet from quite far off, so I slipped away from the high table, scooted in a wide arc and intercepted him.

'Psst!'

Rodden looked around and saw me hiding behind an oak. He gave me a curious look.

I waved him over. 'Where have you been?' I hissed.

He instantly looked annoyed. 'Well, I would tell you, but I've just remembered it's none of your business.'

'Don't be so snippy. What was going on this morning? Were we being attacked?'

Rodden looked around. We weren't far from the others. 'Will you keep your voice down?' he said, through gritted teeth. 'I told you, it's none of your –'

'Yes, yes, none of my business. I didn't want to talk to you about that, anyway. I want to make a deal with you.'

He folded his arms. 'You don't have anything I want.'

'Oh, really? The other day you said you wanted my hand in marriage.'

'That was just to see the look on your face.'

'And how was it?'

'Priceless.'

I could only imagine.

'Well?'

I took a deep breath. 'I know too much. You want me gone. I'll go home if you keep Lilith safe.'

'I don't follow.'

'Come on! It's easy. I'll go quietly back to Amentia, not tell anyone about what you are and what you're doing –'

'You don't know what I'm doing.'

'That's beside the point. You're up to no good, and if I had five minutes in your room I'd find out what. But I promise never to even think of you again, if you, when the time comes, whatever it involves, will make sure that Lilith is far, far away from any trouble.' There. It was exactly what he wanted. He would have to agree.

He shook his head. 'I can't.'

'What do you mean, you can't? You run this place and you can't see that my sister conveniently goes on holiday before things get blown sky-high?'

'That's correct.'

His coolness angered me. It was my sister's life we were talking about, and he was acting as if I was asking him to pass the salt. I gave up bargaining and resorted to threats. 'Yes, you can. You will. Or I'm going to stay and kick up a fuss about the ring. About everything.'

'Suit yourself. No one will believe you. And it's not as if you'll find any evidence now. I've been more careful since I found you under my bed.'

Threats weren't working. I tried to appeal to his humanity; what was left of it, at any rate. 'Where's your compassion? Have the Lharmellins taken it all?'

I could see this was irritating him rather than persuading him. He pitched his voice low and leaned towards me. 'If you're so noble and good,' he said, 'why haven't you told everyone what I am already? Or what you suspected about yourself even before you got in that carriage? Why would you keep such things to yourself? Could it possibly have been because it was in your own best interests?'

'I didn't know what I was getting myself into. Getting everyone into.'

'Rubbish. You've been suffering the hunger for years. And you don't know why, do you? Let me guess. It started when you were twelve, thirteen? Mild at first, but it has increased as you've travelled northwards?'

It had started around the time of my first bleeding. How did he know such a thing? But Lilith was foremost in my mind.

'So you won't help me?'

He studied my face. 'Can you even make it back to Amentia? You've come so close to Lharmell. There will be a lot of pain if you try to leave.'

I nodded. I would try, for Lilith's sake. I had felt a little of that pain already. As long as I had laudanum I would be able to make it.

'And if I try to make sure that Lilith's safe, you'll go home quietly?'

'Promise. You need to *promise* she'll be safe.'

'I can't promise anything. But between Amis and me, she should be safe.'

I nodded. I trusted Amis.

Rodden was grave for a moment, and then gave me a rueful smile. 'You've given me quite a run for my money. You might even be strong enough to stay put in Amentia, what do you think?'

That was rich, considering he was the one who'd drawn me here. 'If I'm left in peace,' I said tartly. But in an odd way, I would miss him. Like a good sparring partner, he seemed to bring out the best in me. Despite the uncertainty and fear of the past weeks, I had felt more alive than I ever had in my life. I was tempted to tell him so as he stood before me, all his sarcasm and prickliness gone. He leaned against the tree, his eyes still on my face. I felt my face grow warm under his gaze, and I couldn't help wondering how it would have been if circumstances were different – if we weren't enemies, for one. 'Rodden . . .' I began.

'Yoo-hoo! Darlings!' It was Rupa. She'd spotted us and was coming over. 'Are we to have another wedding before the year is out?' She thought she'd caught a pair of lovers in a tryst behind a tree.

He bowed. 'Perhaps, madam,' he said, and offered me his arm.

I thought Rodden would disappear as soon as I was seated back at the table, but he sat down next to me. We kept a careful silence for a while, but the beautiful day and festive mood softened us, and I soon found he was passing me dishes and filling my glass as if we were the lovers Rupa had flushed from the garden.

'Where are Leap and Griffin?' he asked.

'In my room. Lilith doesn't like them much so I thought it best they didn't come to the wedding.'

'Call them down.'

'They're too far away. They won't hear me.'

'With your mind. Like I showed you.'

I looked at him doubtfully. I hadn't tried the mind-calling thing again. I didn't believe I could do it.

'Go on,' he urged. 'Close your eyes if it helps. Picture them as if you're in the same room, show them a picture of where you are, and ask them to come to you.'

I closed my eyes. In my mind's eye I saw them in my room; Leap curled up on the bed, Griffin nodding off on the bedpost. *The gardens*, I thought with all my might. *Come to the gardens?* They both sat up and looked around, as if hearing something far off. Then the picture faded.

'Did it work?' he asked.

I looked around. 'You tell me.' I felt silly and stabbed my fork into some beans. Then the court gave a collective gasp and I looked up to see Griffin flying low over the tables, fast as an arrow. She wheeled and dove again. With each pass the gasps grew louder. Then Rodden threw a quail into the air and she caught it in her talons, and everyone applauded.

I heard a trill at my feet and looked down. Big green eyes stared up at me. 'Leap!' He jumped into my lap and started sniffing at my plate. I looked at him in wonderment. 'It actually worked.'

Rodden shrugged. 'Of course.' He made it sound as if it was the most natural thing in the world.

'Rodden!' King Askar stood, brandishing a wine glass. He looked a little drunk. 'There you are, my boy. I've just remembered: you promised to give that pretty girl whatever she desired, and the poor thing has had nothing from you.'

I raised my hand and opened my mouth, about to explain about the ring, but Rodden grabbed it and held it under the table. Oh, right. It was a secret.

'Your Majesty,' said Rodden. 'We were just discussing it. In honour of her departure with her mother, Zeraphina would like a ball, the day after tomorrow. A masquerade ball.'

A dance? If I wished for anything it wouldn't be a silly dance. But, as usual, Rodden had made it impossible for me to protest as the king and court were already laughing and clapping their approval.

Rodden was still holding my hand under the table. I was surprised that his touch didn't make me uncomfortable; I didn't shy away, afraid that he could sense what I was through his skin. But then, he already knew. Again, I felt myself wishing things had been different between us. I wouldn't have to hide my true nature from a man who already knew what I was.

'I would have preferred a new bow,' I said quietly, pulling my hand from his grasp. There was no point wishing for something that could never be.

'Most girls prefer dances.'

'I'm not most girls.'

'I've noticed,' he said, looking at the hand I'd taken from him, now resting on the table.

I sat back, gazing around at the tables. Everyone was having such a good time, talking and laughing. Celebrating. Lilith and Amis were in a crowd of well-wishers, opening pretty coloured gifts. Renata had been cornered by the aunts, but she didn't look too upset about it. The four were screeching away about something. Rodden and I were conspicuous by our subdued manner, the only ones talking and eating quietly.

Rodden followed my gaze around the party.

'I wish you would just tell me what was going on. I'd feel much better about leaving Lilith if I knew.'

'I've told you that I'll guard her. You'll have to be content with that.'

'But if I only knew I might be able to put it out of my mind.'

'You're reasoning makes no sense,' he scoffed.

'Yes, it does. I'm a very curious person. I'd be able to forget about –'

'Drop it, Zeraphina.' The frown had returned to his brow.

I was silent until Carmelina took me away for a walk. 'I had to get away from that table. I was eating myself into oblivion! And you looked like you needed rescuing from Rodden. He looks so morbid today,' she said when we were out of earshot.

'Yes, he's in a bad mood. As usual. Thanks.' We walked towards the sundial on the far side of the grounds.

'When I looked over earlier you were chatting quite nicely. What happened?' She was needling me for gossip. Ever since Rodden announced the tournament people had been whispering about a secret engagement.

'We don't really chat. We've reached a sort of understanding, I guess.'

'What, he gives you your ring back and you stop telling everyone he's a spy?'

I reddened. I'd forgotten my outburst to Carmelina at the markets. 'Something like that,' I muttered.

Carmelina gave me a sidelong glance. 'You know, I think I'll miss you, Zeraphina. You're the most interesting thing to happen around here for a long time. That tournament! My heart was in my mouth the whole time. At first I thought he was going to let you win, but you should have seen the strain on his face. He must really want to marry you.' Carmelina flopped down on a bench, eyeing me carefully.

I plucked a yellow flower and began tearing it to shreds. 'No. He just wanted to win, same as me.' I wanted to tell Carmelina that if she was bored after I left, all she needed to do was look up into the night sky. The Lharmellins certainly weren't going to bore anyone.

'Excuse me, ladies.'

I turned and saw Rodden.

'I was hoping I could borrow Zeraphina for a moment.'

'Oh, borrow away.' Carmelina flashed me a knowing smile.

He held out his arm, and after a moment I took it. Carmelina was being a pain, anyway.

Rodden led me away from the feast into a darker part of the grounds where I'd never been before. The laughter and voices disappeared behind us, muffled by distance and foliage. I could hear only the twittering of birds. I wondered if I should be afraid, but Rodden had that look on his face, the one he'd had earlier when we'd just been ourselves, and not enemies.

'Where are you taking me?'

'Shh,' he admonished.

We didn't seem to be on any sort of path, and had to keep ducking under ferns and trailing willows as we made our way into thicker undergrowth. Just before Rodden pulled away a palm frond, he turned to me and put his finger to his lips.

We stepped into a little glade. The sunlight filtered through the canopy and lay dappled on the grass. He stood behind me, hands on my shoulders, directing my gaze.

'Wait,' he murmured.

Then, out of the darkness, shy as anything, stepped a beautiful blue bird. It was the peacock. With dainty steps it made its way to the middle of the glade, its feathery golden tail trailing over the grass. It paused, as if posing for us. Then it slowly raised its tail and it spread like a fan. I gasped, despite the caution to be silent. It was even more beautiful close up. Hundreds of blue and green eyes shimmered in the afternoon light. The peacock stood for a moment, as if knowing it was being admired, and then slowly lowered its tail and disappeared back into the bushes.

'Oh, it's so beautiful,' I cried, turning to Rodden. 'It doesn't seem real. It's like somebody crafted it out of jewels and feathers.'

Rodden was smiling down at me, and I sensed unspoken words.

'What?' I asked.

He shook his head and led me back to the wedding feast. By the time we were nearing the tables, I felt my good mood seep away. Lilith. Lharmell. It all came rushing back to me. Rodden must have seen the look on my face because he stopped and turned to me.

'Did you forget? Just for a moment?' He nodded his head in the direction we had come.

I realised he was referring to the peacock. I had forgotten the whole sorry mess, just for a moment. I grinned up at him. 'Yes, I did. For the very first time.' He smiled too, and we were smiling at each other out of genuine happiness. That was a first too. And then I realised, looking at him, I had forgotten again. And I began to laugh.

———

Just as Renata had predicted, there was a bedsheet hanging in the great hall the next morning, proof to everyone that Lilith had been a virgin on her wedding night. I sat next to her on the dais and helped myself to fruit.

'I'm so embarrassed,' Lilith hissed. 'Do you think they can take it down yet?' She looked a little pink but happy, too.

I gave her a nudge. 'How was it?' She'd been as white as her flimsy nightgown when everyone had crowded into Amis's bedchamber the previous night to tuck in the bride and groom.

Lilith blushed again and smiled. 'It was . . . nice. I mean, I knew what to expect, sort of, but at the same time I didn't. Hush now, Amis is coming.'

As Amis came up to the high table, everyone gathered in the hall erupted into lewd cheers and catcalls. Lilith ducked her face behind her hand.

Rodden hadn't appeared yet and I desperately wanted to talk to him. Before the applause died down, I slipped away and out a side door, making my way to the northern turret. At the top of the stairs, I knocked on the banister to announce my arrival, and to prove that I wasn't there to snoop.

'What?' came the response.

'It's, uh, just me.' I came into the room.

Rodden was at his desk poring over some books which he immediately closed. 'I told you. I hid all the evidence.'

'Very funny.' I sat on the edge of his desk, peering at the spines of the books. He turned them away from me. 'Sorry,' I said. 'Habit.'

'What do you want?' It seemed Rodden had given up brooding just for the wedding and now he was back to his normal, irate self.

'I need a favour.'

'Now, there's a surprise.'

'Why are you always so grumpy?'

'Why are you always so annoying?'

I shrugged. 'Enjoy it while you can. I'll be gone the day after tomorrow.'

He sat silently, his arms folded. Waiting.

'I need you to get me some of that laudanum stuff. A big bottle. Enough to knock me out till I get to Amentia.'

'Certainly not. Laudanum is highly addictive. You'll be hooked after a week. I thought you said you were strong enough to do this.'

'Conscious you mean? Are you joking? I go into cold sweats just thinking about it.'

'You have to try. You can't take laudanum for the rest of your life. You'll turn into a zombie.'

'A zombie is better than a harming.'

He narrowed his eyes at me. 'You have no idea what you're talking about.'

'Then tell me and I will.'

He sighed. We were back to that old argument.

When he spoke again his voice was softer. 'You forgot yesterday. Twice. I could see it in your eyes.'

I looked at my hands in my lap. At the rings on my thumbs. Yesterday, I had forgotten because of him. 'I don't think I can do it by myself.'

'Come on, Zeraphina. You're stronger than that.'

I looked out an arrow slit. I could see the sea from this height; the northern horizon.

'Oh, all right,' he said. He went to the bench. There was the clink of glass as he searched among various bottles. He came back and put a very small vial into my hand. 'It's enough for one dose. Swallow it just before you get into the carriage. All of it at once. And don't tell your mother.' He closed my hand around it. 'And then try to forget everything. Marry someone in the south. Far, far to the south.'

I nodded. 'Thank you.'

He held my hand for a moment longer. 'All right.' He looked back to his books and I knew I'd been dismissed. I hovered for a moment, wondering if that was it; if the last time I ever saw him I would be looking at the top of his head. 'Bye,' I muttered, and turned away.

I emerged at the bottom of the stairs, tucking the tiny bottle of oblivion into my sleeve.

———

I was sitting on the terrace when the knock came at the door. It was the morning of the ball being thrown in my honour, and I was trying to come up with a way of getting out of it. I wasn't in the mood for a dance. A book lay forgotten in my lap and a cold glass of water was sweating at my elbow. Leap was basking in the sun, belly-up to catch the rays. Griffin had disappeared, but in my mind's eye I could see her circling over the wilderness that grew to the north of the grounds. I was getting better at this mind-communication thing. It would be my one comfort on the journey home, after the laudanum had worn off.

'Zeraphina!' Renata called. 'There's something here for you.'

A huge paper box was perched on the ottoman, done up with a gold ribbon.

'Who is it from?' I asked.

'How should I know?'

I pulled the ribbon off and opened the box. Underneath layers of tissue was a mask: it was a costume for the masquerade ball. Renata had already found me a plain silver mask to wear with one of my dresses, but this was something else. It was heavy and golden, and instead of a nose it had a beak. From the eye-holes dripped tears of diamonds.

Underneath the mask was a dress, and I pulled it out. It was of the richest blue satin, with a tailored bodice like an Amentine gown and a long train. The train was made of golden feathers, dotted with hundreds of blue and green eyes. 'It's a peacock costume.' I thought of the creature's plaintive cries, so beautiful and yet so sad. The diamond tears on the mask made sense now.

'I can see that. Who is it from?'

There was no note. But I knew. 'It's from Rodden.'

'Oh, really.' She pursed her lips. 'Doesn't he know that only the male peacocks are blue? Peahens are brown.'

I shrugged, transfixed by the beautiful dress. 'It doesn't matter. It's just a costume.' I took the whole package to my room and closed the door. As soon as I'd seen the dress I'd known what Rodden was trying to tell me: the peacock was a reminder that I could put the Lharmellins out of my mind if I really wanted to. It was strange that he'd drawn me northwards only to want to send me back almost immediately. Strange and infuriating. But I had his assurance that he and Amis would keep Lilith safe, and their union meant my people wouldn't starve.

I still didn't have the answers I craved. But with these comforts, and the tiny bottle of laudanum to help me, I could find the strength to go home.

ELEVEN

Now that Lilith was safely married, my mother could turn to her Next Big Project: me.

'You haven't met nearly enough men,' she reproached as Eugenia expertly did my hair. She swept my hair off my neck into a twist, and little golden clips studded with blue-green jewels were placed among my curls.

'I've met men. I nearly married one. Don't you remember?' I turned my head this way and that, admiring the sparkling clips in the mirror. I often felt detached from the whole affair of dressing for dinner and parties, as if I were a doll, but I found tonight was different. I wanted to do justice to the dress. It was strapless, the bodice peacock-blue and edged in gold, full skirted at the front and gathered into an elaborate, foaming bustle of satin and peacock feathers at the back. I insisted that every inch of bare skin was powdered with gold: my shoulders, décolletage, and the lower part of my face. The golden mask would cover my eyes, and my lips were painted with more gold. I carried a golden fan that, when it was opened, revealed hundreds of eyes and looked exactly like a peacock's tail. It belonged to Queen Ulah, and she'd insisted I borrow it when she heard about my costume. I opened it and practised fluttering it coquettishly.

Renata wasn't amused by my comment. 'How could I forget, Daughter? You were a cat's whisker away from life as a politician's wife.' She said this as if it were the most loathsome thing in the world. I remembered how she treated her own politicians: like something to be scraped off a shoe. 'Amis's aunts have some unmarried sons. Prince Phillip sounds like a very sweet young man. Calli and I will introduce you tonight.'

'I'm not marrying a Pergamian,' I insisted. It would be too close to Lharmell for my comfort.

Renata fastened on my mask and stepped back to look at me. 'Turn, darling, turn.'

I turned, and all the gold dust and jewels sparkled

in the candlelight. The dress made pleasant swishing sounds on the floor.

'I don't like to say this about my own daughter as it's rather conceited of me, but you are stunning.' She frowned. 'So why is it crying? The mask I mean.'

I looked in the mirror at the glittering tears that the bird, that I, was shedding. 'Because it's sad?'

Renata's frown deepened. 'You'd better stay far away from that Rodden Lothskorn tonight. I don't want you near him.'

'Whyever not?'

'Because he's in love with you. Now, come on. Let's go and find this prince.' Renata pulled her own black mask over her eyes and we made our way to the ballroom.

I allowed myself a secret smile. Now that Rodden was forbidden to see me, he was sure to turn up. I don't know why I should care if he was there or not. But it would be an awful pity if he missed seeing the dress.

The great hall was a heaving, swirling, mad rush of colours and unfamiliar people. The chandeliers had been lowered to just above the reach of the dancers and the walls had been strung with gold ribbons and baubles. The alacrity with which the Pergamians were able to throw party after party amazed me.

I had my fan open and fluttering the minute I stepped into the room; it was incredibly hot. As we moved through the anonymous mass of people, first a poodle, then a seahorse, and then some sort of bird of paradise screeched my name and kissed me. They must have recognised me from the archery tournament, but I had no idea who they were or how they knew me in my costume. A clutch of pretty swans waved to me, and I thought perhaps they were the teenage girls who'd smiled shyly at me as they'd taken their marks at the tournament.

I suddenly felt like the guest of honour after all. I was quite pleased with myself for having made such an impression in less than a fortnight.

'Yoo-hoo! Renata! Over here.' It was Calli, standing at the refreshments table. She held a napkin in her palm loaded with canapés. Next to her stood a young man in white satin with a mass of cotton wool on his head. When he saw me he gasped and clutched my hand.

'My dear, you look absolutely gorgeous.'

'Thank you, ah . . . Phillip?'

'Yes, Princess, this is my son,' Calli interjected. 'Doesn't he look adorable?'

I looked at the man again, wondering what he could be. 'Whipped cream?' I guessed.

'He's a cloud, silly! A cloud!' screeched Calli, and her pink tiered dress bounced up and down. She, it seemed, was dressed as a cake.

'Phillip, why don't you get Zeraphina some punch and take her out on the terrace?' suggested Renata.

I didn't want punch on the terrace, I wanted to stay right where I was and play spot the harming. But Renata gave me a hard look, so I accepted the cup and Phillip's arm and we made our way outside where it was blissfully cool.

'The cloud thing was Mother's idea. I wanted to be a stallion but she thought I didn't have the figure for it.'

He was a tiny bit plump, but it was nothing a horse costume wouldn't cover. 'Oh, I didn't choose my costume either,' I said airily. I took a big gulp of punch. It was very good indeed. Some sort of exotic fruit mixture, I guessed. I drained the glass.

'Yes, but yours is perfect.' He was looking through the windows to the dance floor, but the gauzy curtains made it very hard to make anyone out.

'Looking for someone?' I asked.

'Yes, a snake and an ostrich. They're my friends, Corrin and Windsor. You'll have to meet them, they're such fun.' He noticed my empty glass. 'Like another?'

'Please.'

As he went I saw him do a double-take on a man dressed in a bullfighter's costume, and then give a blacksmith an admiring glance. It occurred to me that perhaps Phillip liked men in the way that girls liked men. Calli and Renata would be disappointed. All the matchmaking in the world wasn't going to do me any good with Phillip.

When he came back I decided to get things moving. I greedily drank half my punch and said, quite loudly, 'So, have you noticed how many bats there are around here?' This sounded like a Dangerous Conversation, and I waited for a dark-haired man to spring out of nowhere and start berating me.

'Why are you shouting? No, can't say that I have. Tell me about the tournament,' he said, eyes aglow. 'It was so thrilling. What's this Lothskorn fellow really like?'

'Arrogant. And a bit of a jerk,' I said, and he looked crestfallen. 'Phillip, don't take this the wrong way, but do you like . . . men?'

He looked around us and said softly, 'I rather have to say that I do, but don't tell Mother, eh?' Through his mask I saw him wink. He elbowed me. 'Dreadfully disappointed, aren't you, that you won't be spending the rest of your life married to a cloud?

Now, come on, you have to tell me. Who do you really like?'

I thought for a moment. 'The Earl of Federna.' He was the large man that Calli had professed to admire at the tea party in Rupa's suite.

Phillip looked at me, stricken with horror. Then he started to laugh. 'You had me for a second there! Oh, you had me! Nice deflection, but I know who you –'

I downed the rest of my punch. 'I might just get some more,' I said, waving my glass.

'He's not by the refreshments. I already checked for you.'

'I don't know what you mean,' I called over my shoulder.

Drat. Why did everybody think they knew all about me just because of some silly competition? I refilled my punch glass and stood in a corner, sipping it. It really was very good punch. I finished the glass and started to feel a bit light-headed. It must have been the heat. I brandished my fan and started flapping it in my face. My eyes scanned the crowd, but I didn't see anyone I knew. Then an ostrich flounced by and I guessed that it was Corrin. Or Windsor.

On an impulse I stepped straight into the dancers and let them carry me off, moving with their tide like a grain of sand on the beach. There were no rigid rows tonight. The musicians were playing some sort of waltz and people danced in pairs or groups or simply moved around erratically, laughing at nothing that I could see. As I moved deeper into the crowd the costumes became more and more grotesque. There was a weasel and a great clawed badger and strange things with long curved noses. A coven of witches cackled and waved their pointed yellow fingernails in the air. I was shoved this way and that by a bevy of court jesters doing some sort of coordinated tumbling routine in the tight space. Heat rose in my cheeks and I felt woozy. I wanted to get out – out into the fresh air where I could *breathe* again. But I was trapped in a mass of people and I couldn't move and I was hot but there wasn't enough room to use my fan and I was being pushed and pulled around by the heaving bodies and people kept screeching and saying my name over and over and I wished they would stop and –

Zeraphina.

And I knew that not-voice. I felt hands on my waist and they turned me, and I was looking up at a dark-haired man in a golden mask with a beak, and he was wearing a peacock-blue jacket.

'I was told you were at the refreshments table,' he said.

My vision cleared, and it was like we were the only people for miles around. All sound and movement fell away as I looked into his blue eyes behind his mask. 'Who said that?'

'A little cloud you ditched.' He took my hand, held it aloft and turned me slowly. I looked back at him over my shoulder, a smile curving my golden lips. My skirts brushed against his legs as I completed the turn.

'Very nice,' he murmured when I was looking up at him again. His hands found my waist again, as if he was holding me apart from the mêlée around us.

'My mother says only male peacocks are blue. The girls are brown.'

'Would you rather have a brown dress?'

I hiccupped.

'Have you been drinking the punch?' he asked.

'Yes, three glasses.'

'Don't have any more.'

'Why?'

'Because now that a weasel, a snake and a swan have been at it, it's more rum than anything else.'

'A little swan, too? And I thought they were such nice girls.'

'Do you want to sit down?'

I didn't feel hot any more, or out of breath. And I didn't want him to let go of me or the world might slide out of control again. 'No!' I said, a little too loudly. 'I want to dance.'

He slid a hand to the small of my back and took one of mine in his, and we were off, whirling with the others. The chandeliers spun overhead. I was smiling, my feet somehow knowing the unfamiliar but simple steps. Now *this* was a dance. My cheek just grazed the shoulder of his dark blue jacket. The punch made me bold, and instead of ducking my head I held his steady blue gaze. We danced on and on, until finally the last strains of music died away.

We came to a stop in a darkened alcove, and though we were hemmed in by the crowd, it seemed as though we were completely alone. His hands were on my waist again, gripping tightly. He stood close, and I tipped my head back so I could look up at him. I saw his eyes drop to my gold-painted mouth, and my breath caught in my throat.

Zeraphina . . .

His voice had no earthly sound. I felt as if I knew him as well as I knew myself. I recognised something within him. I remembered Amis's vows. *Because deep down, we're the same . . .*

His hands slid to caress my back. I felt a sweet-sharp tug on my insides. He must have felt it too as his eyes flared in response. And then his mouth descended on mine. I fell into the kiss, my hands smoothing up his chest. In my mind's eye I saw a blazing thread running between us, taut and humming. I not only saw it, but felt it and heard it, too; it hummed on a sweet frequency, like the yearning notes of a violin.

He pulled back and looked at me in astonishment, his lips parted. Then his eyes dropped to my neck, curved and exposed. We were breathing heavily and I felt his breath on my bare shoulders.

He ducked his head and I felt his lips just graze my throat. I was drunk not on the punch now, but intoxicated by his nearness.

A thought brushed the edge of my consciousness with frantic, beating wings, and I frowned slightly. Was there something I was forgetting?

Because deep down, we're the same . . .

I felt his breath again on my throat, and the gentleness of his lips became a hard pressure.

The warmth that radiated through my body condensed suddenly, becoming a cold, hard mass of fear.

He's going to bite me!

My eyes snapped open. The spell cast by the evening and the dress suddenly fell away. What was I doing, kissing a man who'd proved again and again that he was not to be trusted. I'd forgotten everything, *just like he wanted me to.*

I tried to pull myself from his grasp, but his hands help me tightly. 'Let go of me!' I cried, and remembered the heavy gold fan that dangled from one wrist. I gripped it, and landed a thwack on his hands. His grip loosened momentarily and I pulled away. I fought to find a way out of the pressing bodies, knowing he was behind me, chasing me. But I was faster, nipping through narrow gaps in the crowd before he could even spot them. I fled the hall, tearing down corridors and quickly losing myself in unfamiliar turns. I could hear him calling my name, his pounding feet. A door, I needed a door in a stone wall. I needed to get away. I finally found a stairwell and tore up it. And then suddenly I was out in the night and under the stars.

I held my breath for a moment, straining for the sound of running feet, but heard nothing. I slumped in relief. A breeze started to blow and I lifted my arms, grateful for the cool air as I was perspiring in my gown. The parapet was spinning so I closed my eyes. I heard a snatch of music and thought the musicians had started up again.

There was a beating sound in the air and a sharp clack like the one Griffin's talons made when she landed on stone.

The music wasn't coming from the great hall. It was floating on the wind; haunting and painfully sweet.

I opened my eyes. I could just make out a large, dark shape.

Griffin? What have you done to yourself?

It looked a lot like Griffin, except this bird stood half as tall as me again. The moon came out and I saw it towering over me; it had the lethal curved beak, sooty feathers and powerful talons of a bird of prey. If I wasn't used to being around eagles I might have had hysterics. But I knew what to be afraid of, and it wasn't a bird. It was a dark-haired, slippery trickster who was after my blood. As I approached, the bird crouched down and I saw that it wore a bridle of sorts, and a saddle was nestled between its wings.

I heard the pounding of footsteps, quickly ascending. He'd found me. Rodden would be out that door at any moment. There was nowhere to run except along the parapet, and I knew he would soon catch me if it came down to an all-out sprint.

I looked at the monstrous eagle crouched down before me. It regarded me with an impatient glassy stare that seemed to say, *On or off? I haven't got all night.*

From within the stairwell, somewhat muffled, I heard my name being called. I had about three seconds until Rodden would be on the parapet. Three seconds was how long it took me to scramble onto the bird's back, grab the reins, and for it to launch itself into the sky.

Rodden's not-voice yowled my name in anguish and I felt a painful yank, as if a cord attached to my insides had been snagged.

The bird was climbing rapidly. Once we were a hundred feet off the ground I had to shut my eyes because of the wind and because the drop terrified me. A shudder went through the bird as if it had stumbled mid-air and I felt another painful yank on my insides.

We levelled off and flew straight. I dared a peek, wondering if from this height we would be face-to-face with the moon. But no, there it was by my left shoulder, still higher in the sky than me. I dared not look at the ground, and I shut my eyes tightly again because they had started to stream in the wind. It was freezing and I huddled close to the bird's back, burying my hands in its thick feathers.

It did occur to me to worry where I was being taken, but I had an inherent trust in birds of prey, and by then we were descending in long, lazy circles. I wondered how far we'd come. To the beach I'd ridden to the day before the tournament? It couldn't have been far as we'd been airborne for such a short time. We landed with a jolt, and with legs like jelly I half-dismounted, half-fell onto the dusty ground. I threw my palms back to brace against the fall, and a searing pain flared where my skin touched the dirt. I scrambled up and furiously rubbed my hands against my skirt, and then stared at them in the dim light. It was too dark to see but I was sure they had been burned. While I was examining my hands the bird flapped its wings and took off.

'Hey, wait!' I called, reaching to it in vain. It was already becoming a speck in the sky.

Drat. It was going to be a long walk back to the palace. Now, which way? The circling descent had muddled my sense of direction. I stood still, listening for the sea, but the place was eerily quiet. I must be in the forest just before the sea then, the one I'd ridden through on the horse that day. There were trees on all sides so I couldn't get a look at the horizon. The ground had a slight gradient, and I reasoned that, being the lowest point of the landscape, the sea must lie downhill. This meant the palace, being in the opposite direction to the sea, would be uphill. I was quite pleased with myself for figuring it out.

I found something that might be a path and started walking up the slope. It was freezing cold and I was losing a lot of heat from my shoulders so I pulled the top skirt of the dress up and over myself like a cloak. That was a little better, but now my legs were getting cold as they were only protected by thin petticoats. I would just have to tough it out for the hour or so that it took me to reach the palace limits.

To keep warm, I thought of all the things I was going to say to Rodden when I saw him: that he was a horrid trickster and an arrogant jerk and not to worry, I was getting in that carriage because the thought of seeing his sneering, smug face ever again made my blood boil. I wished I had seen his face as the bird had launched itself into the air. What a hoot!

Still chuckling to myself, I looked around and for the first time I noticed that something was wrong. The trees were barren. There was no grass or shrubs, either. Just dust. I reached down and touched the ground with my finger, and again a stinging pain shot through my arm. I wiped the finger on my petticoat. That was very odd, and inconvenient as well as my shoes were starting to pinch. Walking barefoot over this ground would be like walking over hot coals. I cast my mind back to the day I'd ridden through here, and I distinctly remembered a lot of greenery, on both the trees and the ground. I was obviously in a different part of the forest. A dead part. I hoped I would get out of it soon, as it was a hellish place. There was no sound except for my own breathing, which was getting louder and louder in my ears. I wished a possum would rattle some branches or an owl would hoot, just to reassure me that the place wasn't entirely dead. Because it definitely felt as if it was.

I looked up at the sky, but yellow-grey clouds had passed over the stars. I realised I was still wearing the peacock mask and I ripped it off, flinging it away from me. What time had it been when I'd fled the ball? Not late. Not much after ten, probably. If I hurried I might be able to get back before Renata missed me. I was shivering now inside the satin. Why had the temperature plummeted so fast? It had been such a hot day, and on the terrace earlier the night air had been pleasantly warm.

After an hour of trudging through the same dead, black forest, I started to worry. Where had that bird taken me? Had we flown east, along the coast?

If so, I could be walking further from the palace, not towards it. I hadn't felt it turn once we were in the air and it had definitely been heading north when we'd taken off.

North. Oh, jeepers. Just how far had the bird taken me? It had felt like barely minutes in the air, but I was a little tipsy and Rodden had just put the wind up me. And the bird had been flying very fast. Fast enough to get me over the Unctium?

Looking around at the alien landscape I felt a rising sense of dread. Barren, black trees. Frigid temperatures. I remembered the large dark shapes with flapping wings circling in the sky above the palace, and how quickly they'd disappeared back across the straits. Big, bird-like things. Like the one I had so rashly climbed aboard. I recalled Rodden's anguished not-voice as we'd leapt into the air. As if I was in great danger. *As if I was being taken to Lharmell.*

Oh, no. Not there. Not *here.*

Suddenly the black forest seemed aglow with twin points of blue light, eyes that stared at me hungrily. I saw that the ground beneath me had flattened out. Bewildered, I was no longer sure of the direction I'd come from. I looked for my footprints but the ground was hard-packed.

Now that I knew I was in Lharmell, not Pergamia, I did a quick rethink. Uphill, away from the sea, would be north here, not south. The way I'd been going was leading me deeper into Lharmell. To reach the straits I would have to go back the way I'd come. If I could get there I could . . . what? Find a boat? I doubted such things existed in this place. I'd seen no signs of civilisation so far.

First things first: my shoes. They would not do. There could be hours of tramping ahead of me, plus the hour or so that I'd added by walking in the wrong direction. I found a rock and touched it to see if it was as hazardous as the ground, but there was no pain. I sat down and pulled off my shoes, carefully tucking my feet under me out of harm's way. Examining the shoes, I thought I could use the soles, but the rest of them would have to go. They were made of a stiff blue satin, perfect for the ballroom but hellish to walk in. I was amazed I'd lasted this far. The satin tore off easily and I worked away at the little heels on the rock until I'd wormed them off. I tied the thin soles to my feet with part of an underskirt, being careful that no parts of my feet were exposed to the poisonous ground.

I stood and tested them out. There were no shooting pains and the binding didn't fall apart straight away. They would do for a little while. I set out in the direction I thought I had come from, gathering my make-shift cloak around me and hoping that a swift pace would soon warm me up. I went more carefully now, running my eyes over the blackness around me, and checking behind to see if I was being followed.

I thought I'd been so clever to jump aboard that bird. But it was stupid. So stupid. There wasn't a lot I could use to defend myself against a Lharmellin. I tried making a staff but the wood was also poisonous. I thought about finding a good-sized stone, but carrying it would weigh me down and I doubted lobbing one measly stone was going to mean the difference between life and death.

After about an hour the ground began to slope erratically and I was no longer sure that I was headed for the ocean. If only there was an opening in the trees and I could see the horizon; that might give me a better idea of where I was headed. Climbing a tree might have helped but it wasn't possible.

Hours went by, possibly three. I trudged across the hard, uneven ground, shivering with cold. I was now lost. As far as I knew, I could be heading into the very heartland of Lharmell. After another hour the temperature plummeted some more but the sky began to lighten, and I looked around, hoping to see something that would set me in the right direction. All I saw were more black-trunked trees, their uppermost branches bare and needle-sharp. The sky lightened to a sickly yellowish-grey. I hoped that when the sun was high enough it would show through the clouds and I could get some sense of direction. And that it would grow a little warmer.

I kept my ears peeled for the flap of wings, hoping that one of those big birds would land and I could get on its back again and somehow steer it back to Pergamia. But there were no sounds. No birds heralding the dawn. They had either been killed by the toxic forest, or else were never here to begin with.

As morning wore on I began to get terribly thirsty. I had seen no water so far and the landscape didn't allow much reason to hope for it. Even if I did find a pond or stream, there was a good chance that it would be poisonous, too.

After another hour, the bindings on my shoes fell apart. I found another rock and hopped over to it, the ground searing my feet where the fabric had disintegrated. Looking at the remains of my foot coverings, it seemed that whatever made the surroundings toxic had eaten through the bindings. What a terrible place this was. I tore fresh strips from my petticoat and rebound my feet. I hoped that I would reach the ocean before I ran out of clothing entirely.

It must have been nearing midday by then, but it had grown no warmer and I searched the sky in vain for the sun. The ominous clouds blotted it out too well for me to see its glow, and I had no shadow. There was nothing to do but press on and hope for the best. I travelled slowly now, dehydration and fatigue making me unsteady. My stomach was growling despite my anxiety. I would have to rest soon, but lying down on the ground was an impossibility.

Sometime in the afternoon when my eyes had grown gritty and blurred and my tongue was stuck to the roof of my mouth, I saw a rocky outcrop. Blindly, I made my way towards it, found a flattish sort of boulder and lay down.

For an instant, it felt a lot better than struggling over the dusty ground. Then it just became hard and uncomfortable. I shifted around until I was only prodded in half a dozen places, and then all I could do was lay there.

And think of water.

Water. I'd taken it for granted my whole life. Whenever I'd needed it all I had to do was reach for it. I chastised myself for all the missed opportunities:

all those times when I could have been drinking water but hadn't. I'd never known that I should have been cherishing it, worshipping it as the elixir of life that it was. Because now that I didn't have it, I was being driven mad. In my mind's eye I saw myself at the high table in Pergamia, picking at all the strange food. On the table sat a goblet, filled to the brim with cold water.

Drink it! I urged my imagined self. *What are you doing, Zeraphina? Drink!*

But that Zeraphina didn't hear me. She went on ignoring the goblet and for some reason I felt more desolate than ever.

For something to do with my tongue, I pulled a clip from my hair, broke off the jewel and put it in my mouth. I sucked on the small stone, trying to get my saliva flowing. It started to work and my mouth was moist for the first time in hours, and I faded into an exhausted sleep.

When I woke it was dark again. How late it was I didn't know, but the sky had cleared up somewhat and through fog I could see a handful of stars. I realised that I would have to trek through the night again and wished that I hadn't slept the day away. I could miss things in the dark, and besides, it was far more terrifying.

I put fresh bindings on my feet and eased myself down from the rock. My body ached all over from the tension and unexpected exercise. Black spots danced before my eyes and my heart thumped painfully in my chest, straining to push my thickened blood around my body. The temperature was almost at freezing and I huddled into the blue satin. There was even less underskirt to protect my legs now. It occurred to me that before I could be captured by Lharmellins I might die of exposure.

As I walked I rubbed my arms with the dress, trying to clean off the gold powder, which was starting to itch.

Half an hour later I felt a faint breeze, one that carried the low rumble of chanting voices. I stood stock-still, listening, my heart thumping more painfully than ever. There came to my ears a sound like a mewling kitten, frightened and alone. In the moonlight I could see a clearing up ahead and something moving around in it, but my fear made me crouch low to the ground instead of approach. I clutched my hands around my knees, trying not to shake or even breathe too loudly.

The mewling reached my ears again, and this time the call sounded like a word, a human word, like *hello* or *help*. I opened my mouth to call back but saw a streak of white-blue light in the distance and clapped a hand over my mouth. There were several more flashes of light, all moving rapidly towards the clearing, as fast as arrows.

Lharmellins.

There must have been at least six of them darting among the trees. They were making an odd clicking noise as they closed in on the clearing. It was an almost gleeful sound, as if they were chuckling to one another.

That's when I realised what was happening. They were hunting, calling to one another as they closed in on their prey.

I pressed my hands even harder over my mouth, willing myself not to make a noise. Whoever it was in the clearing was crying now, calling out in fright. I could do nothing but stare helplessly as a Lharmellin shot into the clearing. In the light from its eyes I saw a boy crouched in the dirt. He shielded himself from the glow with his arm and sobbed. The Lharmellin threw back its head and clicked again, and, so fast that they were a blur, eight more materialised and surrounded the boy. They didn't appear to walk, but slid over the ground, their dark hooded cloaks trailing over the dirt.

I saw them reach for the cowering figure with long, thin fingers, and I buried my face in my knees, shaking with silent tears. The boy screamed once more, frantic and high pitched, and then was silent.

The only noise was a faint, appreciative clicking as the Lharmellins fed.

I still had my face buried in my skirt when I heard a loud, questioning click at my elbow. I looked up and saw a Lharmellin a few feet away, staring at me, its head cocked to one side. This close I could see its needle-like teeth stained red, the skeleton grin on its features. Its eyes were glowing white-blue and I felt myself bathed in their unnatural light. The thing was very tall and thin, only its twisted grey hands and face visible beneath its cloak. Up close I could see it didn't possess feet, but a thick tail, like a worm.

I scrambled to my feet and backed away.

The Lharmellin raised its chin and clicked again, louder this time. Its companions, who were dozens of feet away, seemed to materialise by its side instantly. They were all looking right at me, their eyes glowing an eerie white-blue. They began their crooning song.

My stomach balled into a fist of dread. *Run!* But I found that I couldn't move. My feet were glued to the spot.

Ever so slowly they began to drift towards me, slithering over the ground, fingers outstretched.

With their tails, and their heads cocked to one side, they looked vaguely reptilian, like curious snakes wondering whether to strike.

I opened my mouth to scream but the sound was frozen in my throat.

TWELVE

I wished fervently that I had died of exposure, because facing the Lharmellins now I saw it would be a far, far better way to go.

There was a flash of gold overhead. Then, in quick succession, three Lharmellins were struck by arrows. They threw back their heads and let out shrieks like an accordion being stepped on, before their bodies collapsed inside their cloaks and they fell into smoking piles.

The other six stopped singing and I found I could move again. I turned and ran. My foot caught on a tree root and I went flying, landing on my forearms in the dirt. Stinging pain shot through my arms.

'Get up! You'll be burned,' a voice snapped.

'I *know*,' I said through gritted teeth. I struggled

up. I hated being told what to do when I was already doing it. It made me furious. Especially when it was him. Because, of course, it was Rodden. He notched up an arrow and fired again, and an answering shriek told me he had hit his mark. The remaining Lharmellins fled, disappearing into the trees. Rodden lowered his bow and looked at me.

What a sight I must have looked, huddled and shivering inside the torn dress, rags on my feet. 'You took your time,' I said, though I hadn't really been expecting to be rescued.

Rodden reached into his pack and pulled out a black cloak, similar to the one he was wearing. In fact it was very similar to the ones the Lharmellins had been wearing. As he wrapped it around me I heard a trill and felt something brush against my legs.

'Leap!' I bent down to scoop him up. 'He's not in pain?' I asked, checking his paws.

'No, this place is only poisonous to humans. Come on, we have to get moving. They'll be back ten-fold.'

I remembered the flash of gold I'd seen just before the arrows had been fired, and looked around for Griffin.

'She'll follow us. There's a cave not far off.'

Among a copse of smaller trees was an entrance to a cave. It didn't look like much from the outside, and wasn't large enough to stand up in, but as we moved further in I saw that it was quite deep. We made a turn, and then another. Rodden stopped and pulled something out of his pack, and an orange glow filled the cave. It was the same coloured glow that I had seen coming from his turret room.

I was about to slump to the ground until I remembered the poisonous dirt. But the floor was rock, and I gratefully slid down, my back against the hard wall.

'Water,' I muttered.

Rodden handed me a flask. 'Just tiny sips,' he said.

As I drank, doing my best not to gulp the water down, I watched Rodden unpacking. He pulled out trousers, a shirt and a pair of boots and stacked them next to me. I looked at the boots with relief. I wouldn't have to trudge all the way back to Pergamia in the remains of my ball shoes.

Finally I could manage to speak. 'They were Lharmellins?' I asked.

Rodden nodded. 'That was them. Endearing creatures, aren't they?'

'They were hunting. They're so *fast*. They killed a boy in the clearing. I think they were about to kill me.'

He shook his head. 'They killed the boy, but they were greeting you. Must have figured you got lost on your way to the tors.'

I was about to ask him about the tors when he pulled something out of his pack that gladdened my heart even more than the boots: my bow. He proceeded to string it and laid it down next to me. I caressed the smooth, shiny wood. Then Rodden pulled out a quiver of arrows but didn't give them to me until he'd also found a pair of gloves that matched the pair he was wearing. He gave me a stern look. 'Never, ever, touch these arrows without these gloves on your hands. They're poisonous to those with Lharmellin blood.'

I frowned. A minute ago he'd said Lharmell was only poisonous to humans. So what was I, human or harming? I put on the gloves. They were very long, reaching all the way up past my elbows.

'Get changed.' He nodded to the stack of clothing next to me and ducked out of sight around the corner.

After a minute of struggling I had to call him back.

'What?'

'I can't get it off.'

'The dress?'

'Yes, and the corset.' I turned my back to him, though I hated to ask him for help.

As he picked at the fastenings he muttered, 'That's right, I forgot you have servants to do this.'

'So would you if you had to go around in this ridiculous get-up all the time.'

Rodden pulled out a knife and cut everything off me. I let out a sigh of relief as the corset loosened. He went away again and I slipped out of the remains of the dress and foot-bindings and put on the shirt and trousers. I marvelled at the clothes. What an odd sensation! I spun around. To have such freedom of movement was invigorating. It also felt illicit to wear such things. What would my mother think?

'I'm done,' I called as I was buckling up the boots.

Rodden sat down opposite me and held out a package. 'Can you eat?'

I grimaced and shook my head. I'd begun to feel trembly and sick. I wrapped the cloak about myself again. It helped a little, but as I tried to relax I felt a tightness in my chest. It radiated outwards, making it difficult to breathe. Not now! I didn't want Rodden to see me collapse in a fit. To distract myself I patted my lap and Leap came over and curled himself against my stomach, a rumbling emanating from deep in his chest. I forced my fingers not to clench in his fur.

'They've got a fix on you,' Rodden said, nodding to Leap and Griffin as he repacked everything into two bags. 'It was the only way I could find you.'

I nodded, my jaw clenched too tightly to speak. I would fight this down. I was a human, not a harming.

'If you'd left me with that ring I could have found you just as easily, but that bird of yours comes in handy. She's a good tracker and scout.'

By now my legs were trembling with the effort not to give in to the pain. Rodden saw the shaking. 'Are you okay?'

I nodded, though I knew it couldn't be very convincing as my eyes were wide and darting around like caged birds.

'No, you're not, you're –'

And then it hit me. I moaned and doubled over. Leap scrambled off my lap. I curled into a ball, pressing my forehead against my knees. This was the worst yet. It felt like someone was dragging white-hot hooks across my insides. From far off I heard

Rodden urging me to be quiet and I realised I was screaming in pain. He pulled me up and held a flask to my lips. What was he doing? I didn't want water at a time like this. The fluid filled my mouth and I swallowed involuntarily. Instantly the pain subsided. Laudanum. He'd given me laudanum. I slumped back with relief.

'Thanks,' I muttered.

He was screwing the cap back on the flask, regarding me warily. 'You're, ah . . . welcome.'

I licked my lips and frowned. Laudanum sure had a funny taste. Sort of thick and tangy, not unpleasant but faintly . . . metallic. My eyes widened. I rubbed the back of my hand across my mouth and looked at it in the dim light. There was a dark red smear on my hand. That wasn't laudanum. That was blood.

My head snapped up. 'You gave me blood?'

'Yes. It's what you needed. You'd die otherwise. What did you think I gave you?'

'Laudanum!'

'That stuff's practically useless. It can only mask the pain for a while, not make it go away.' He was so cool, so logical.

I flew at him and beat him with my fists. 'I don't want to drink blood! Do you hear me? It's vile! It's inhuman!'

He grabbed my wrists and pushed me back. 'You need to keep your voice down,' he growled. 'There'll be dozens of Lharmellins in the area.'

'I don't care!' I hollered. 'I'd rather be dead than live like this.'

He clamped a hand over my mouth. 'If they catch us they will torture your cat and your bird to death. So shut the hell up.'

I wasn't sure if he was telling the truth about Leap and Griffin, but the look in his eye made me fall silent.

He grabbed his bow and quiver and stood up. 'Stay here.' After five minutes he came back. 'There's nothing out there. But you need to keep quiet, because they'll be coming.'

I watched Leap and Griffin, so perfect in the lamplight. Their eyes shone like stars, one pair green, one pair gold. So vivid and alive. I loved them dearly. If Rodden hadn't needed them to track me down they would be safely in Pergamia right now. I hoped they weren't going to die because of me.

'It wasn't human blood, was it?' I asked as he sat down opposite me.

'No. Rabbit.' He stretched his legs out, his left thigh warm against my own.

I remembered the hutch in his room. 'The ones in your turret?'

He nodded.

'Oh.' I couldn't help the small cry of dismay, remembering how sweet they were.

He sighed. 'Yes, I know. They're hideously cute and trusting. I'm a monster.'

'No, they're . . . it's not – it's okay,' I finished lamely. Why on earth was I trying to comfort him? It *was* monstrous.

'I'm glad you think so. You'll need your own set-up like that when we get back. Rabbits are the best. They breed like, well, rabbits, and the turnover is quick so you don't have enough time to get attached to them. And one is just the right amount of blood.'

I grimaced, wondering how many small creatures he'd gone through in his quest to find one that was 'just right'. 'Before, you said this place was only poisonous to humans. So if I'm human why would I need blood?'

'Because you're not all human. You're a part-harming. You've tasted Lharmellin blood but you haven't gone through the Turning. That's what you're being drawn northwards for.'

'What's a Turning?'

'It's a ceremony. It makes you into a full harming. After, you don't feel the pain any more if you try to go south.'

'But?'

'But Lharmell will become your home. The Lharmellins your masters. You won't be Zeraphina any more, but something wicked. Without conscience.'

I shuddered. 'I don't think I want to go to a Turning. Is that what you are, a full harming?'

He snorted. 'I am *not*. I'm a part-harming, like you are.'

'Oh. But you are wicked and unconscionable?'

'I *have* made a good impression,' he muttered.

I narrowed my eyes. 'I noticed you don't deny the charges.'

He put his hand on his heart. 'Any wickedness or lack of conscience that I possess can be attributed only to my flaws of character. I swear.'

'Drat. I was looking forward to the day you would be tried for treason.'

He laughed.

'But I have no recollection of meeting one of these creatures,' I said, turning back to the matter at hand. 'How did this happen to me?'

He considered this. 'I think you should ask your mother.'

I remembered Renata's white face when I'd mentioned Lharmell. The odd story about the sickness. There was something she wasn't telling me. Had she known what I was all along, and kept it from me? How could she do such a thing?

'Do all harmings have pale eyes and black hair?

He nodded. 'We also need blood to survive and have uncontrollable urges to return "home". I was hoping you were going to overcome yours and get in that damned carriage, but here you are.'

I was indignant at that. 'If you wanted me to go home so badly, why did you draw me here in the first place? I know you're the phantom.'

'The what?'

'The thing in my room. All I could see was your eyes. You stole my ring.'

'I took the ring to track you. I wanted to be sure that if you were coming to Pergamia that you would actually get there. There are harmings all over Brivora keeping an eye out for little lost souls like you.'

'So you didn't actually draw me northwards?'

'No. That was the Lharmellins.'

'But why pretend you did?' I asked, exasperated.

He smiled. 'You were just so convinced I was the bad guy. If you wasted time spying on me I thought it would keep you distracted from Lharmell until it was time for you to go home.'

'And the archery tournament?'

'I was curious about how good you were with that bow and arrow. We rate skilled archers very highly in Pergamia. They're our best defence against the harmings that come to steal our people for blood. And again, it was to distract you from Lharmell. And to see the look on your face when I threw in the bit about marrying me.' He laughed.

'You laugh now, but hasn't your plan rather . . . backfired? You had me so convinced you were the bad guy I had to jump on a giant bird to get away from you.'

'Yes, perhaps I did lay it on a bit thick.' He looked at his hands. 'I admit I was rather enjoying myself.' A smile quirked the corners of his mouth. 'I was so angry when I found you in my room, but you should have seen your face when you told me you would be watching *me* from then on. I knew what you were the minute I saw you, that you were like me, and you seemed so fierce, so . . . human, that it gave me hope. It's lonely when you think you're the only person like you in the world. I thought if I could get you far enough away without finding out anything about harmings, then you might not need the blood.

You might not feel like a monster for the rest of your life. Ignorance is bliss, as they say.'

'Oh Rodden,' I muttered. 'I already did feel like a monster – *do* feel like one. Telling me would have helped, don't you see?'

He nodded. 'It was stupid of me. But I wanted to give you the chance that I never –' He stopped himself, shaking his head. 'When you collapsed after the tournament I thought I might just tell you the nice things. The one nice thing. The mind communication with Leap and Griffin. You'll get better at it with time. Because you're so close you'll be able to sense what they're thinking.'

I looked at them both, watching us intently as if they really were following the conversation. Being able to talk to them, as it were; that would be a great comfort.

'The man at the tournament. Was he a harming?'

Rodden's face grew hard. 'Yes. I wanted to kill him as soon as I saw him. I couldn't believe his audacity, competing right there in front of everybody. Harmings are usually more secretive. And you! Running off by yourself. I couldn't believe how stupid you were.'

'Maybe if someone hadn't kept me in the dark for so long I would have known better.'

'Touché.'

'What did you say to him?'

'I told him to back off. That you were with me. It's sort of an honour to guide one of our kind home.'

I grimaced. 'I wish you'd stop saying home.'

'To Lharmell, then.'

'How did you find me in Amentia?' I was afraid that if he stopped talking I might never get him to start again.

'You are full of questions. Don't you want to get some rest?'

I shook my head. It was amazing how quickly I'd recovered. My senses felt sharp and I wasn't sleepy in the least, or hungry. I realised it was because of the blood and tried to feel dismayed, but the intoxication obliterated any guilt. 'Tell me how you found me,' I insisted.

He looked at me from beneath his lashes. 'I heard you.'

'Go on.'

'You were making such a racket, for months on end. I'd never heard anything like it. All the resistance you were putting up to the Lharmellins, the blood-hunger. I heard it all the way in Pergamia, and I was curious. I can travel out of my body. I was taught to do it a long time ago. It's useful for travel-ling long distances.'

I imagined him sitting in his turret room, hearing me rail against the hunger. I'd thought the whole time I'd been alone. 'How long ago did you hear me? How many times did you visit?'

'Oh . . . Once or twice . . .'

He'd known my name. He'd spoken it like it was as familiar as his own. At least, I thought he had. But it was too intimate to put into words. So I changed the subject. 'Tell me what you're doing in Pergamia.'

'You know what I'm doing. Fighting the Lharmellins.'

'But what specifically? What's with all the equipment in your room?'

He gave me a long look.

'Well, come on!' I said. 'We can't have any secrets now.'

'No, it's not that. I'm just choosing my words. Trying to be tactful.'

'That's not like you.'

'How true. Have you ever wondered why such a big, glorious nation like Pergamia would form an alliance with a tin-pot country like yours?'

I rolled my eyes. 'You Pergamians are so full of yourselves. And what happened to being tactful?'

'As you said, not in my nature. And I'm not Pergamian. When the king showed me the letter from your mother, the one outlining a possible alliance with Amentia, there was something in it that caught my interest.'

'The harming sister?'

'It's not always about you, Zeraphina.'

I scowled. 'I was kidding. You're always so serious.'

'And you're always so –'

'All right, all right. The letter. What was in it?'

'Your mother mentioned the Teripsiin Mountains. They're full of metals: tin, iron, copper and so on.'

'Yes, Renata told us that would interest Pergamia.'

'Not those metals.' Rodden picked up the lamp that was giving off the orange glow. 'This is yelbar. It's an alloy of yelinate and bennium. Both are extremely rare elements and are never found together in nature. But when you artificially fuse them you get a metal that, while innocuous to humans, is lethal to Lharmellins and harmings.' He picked up an arrow. I saw that its tip was glowing faintly too. 'These have yelbar in the tip, hence the disintegration of our little friends out there. As we have Lharmellin blood they're toxic to you and me, so don't touch them with your bare hands, and for heaven's sake be careful where you fire them. Don't shoot yourself in the foot, for instance, because you'll crumple up like a burning leaf. You'd be wise to keep your gloves on at all times.'

'So we can be killed the same way as a Lharmellin, but Lharmell is still poisonous to us?' I held up my hands, reddened by contact with the dirt.

Rodden pulled a small pot of salve out of his pack and gave it to me. 'Here, use this on your burns. A human in Lharmell would be dead in hours. But as you've seen, they don't last that long.'

I grimaced, thinking of the Lharmellins clicking to each other as they hunted. I rubbed the salve on and the burning subsided. 'And if we're not in Lharmell we get driven crazy by the urge to come here,' I continued. 'Bit of a paradox, don't you think?'

'I'd never really thought about it that way. But you're right.'

'Can't we reverse it somehow?'

He shook his head. 'I've searched for a way ever since I came to Pergamia. I've collected every book with even the vaguest mention of Lharmell, but I've never found a way to free myself. I'm still looking, but . . .'

'You're not hopeful,' I finished.

'No.'

There was no way out. No way to go back to being a normal human girl, the way I was before the hunger started.

I pressed my face into my hands. 'Then what the hell is the point?'

'Part-harmings don't last long in the wild, so to speak. The urge to go north is so strong they can't ignore it. You're the first one I've met, other than myself, who's been able to resist.'

'How?'

'I don't know.'

I gave a short laugh. Able to resist? 'Haven't you realised where we are? Look around. This is Lharmell. Some resistance.'

He waved my comment away. 'You were drunk, and you thought you had to get away from me. And then you called down that blasted brant.'

'Brant?'

'That huge bird of prey. It's a rider-brant, trained by the Lharmellins. They breed them in the tors.'

'How did I call it down?'

'You were giving off all these need-to-get-away signals, so it helpfully obliged.'

'Oh.'

'Quite. Lharmellins don't use words, they use thought-patterns. Pictures. Yours are quite strong for a part-harming and you let them go zipping off in all directions.'

'And you don't?'

'No. I was trained. Anyway, I was telling you about that letter. The Teripsiin Mountains, as I subsequently discovered, are a rich source of yelinate, which is why your country is suffering so much. The Lharmellins can sense it and they're trying to freeze out anyone who attempts to mine it. All the chanting they do, it's to call the harmings home, but it's also to draw the ice down from the sky. They thrive in the cold.'

I interrupted. 'The Lharmellins are the reason my country is freezing?' I thought of the empty granaries, the famine that could easily seize my country and the cold that had been going for decades. They had caused this? I grew angry. Why was no one doing anything to stop this? A whole country full of people could die. Rodden said he was fighting them, but what had he really done?

'I'm afraid so. Amentia has always had hard winters, but there's something strange happening. The Lharmellins seem to be getting stronger. I can't be sure, but I think they have a new leader. A smart one. The cold is spreading. Soon the Lharmellins will be able to travel out of Lharmell instead of needing the harmings to do their legwork. The harmings carry vials of Lharmellin blood about the countryside, infecting humans. They also kidnap people for their blood, taking them home to Lharmell, like that boy you saw. Then they dump the bodies back where they came from. You were right about something happening on the morning of Lilith's wedding. A dozen bodies were found at the docks, all bloodless.

I shuddered. 'But why are they doing this?'

'They're our natural predators and they want to expand their territory. I can't be sure exactly because the records are sketchy, but once, a long time ago, the world was colder and I think the Lharmellins existed outside Lharmell. They want that territory back. There are already more harmings than ever, and places like Amentia are getting dangerously cold. As soon as the Lharmellins can leave Lharmell, we're pretty much done for.' He got up and went to check the cave mouth.

I didn't want to live in pain and hunger for the rest of my life – which might not be very long, according to Rodden – and I certainly didn't want to become a harming. I thought of Lilith, not far away across the straits, with brants circling over the keep every night. How long until something happened to her?

When he came back he said, 'It will be dawn in about an hour. We'll go then.'

'Go where?'

'Pergamia of course. We'll call a brant down and make our escape. It's safer when it's light. The slightly warmer air makes the Lharmellins sluggish.'

'We're just going to leave? We need to do something. Kill that leader that's getting things organised. Buy ourselves some time.'

'No,' he said, with exaggerated patience. 'I need to get you across the straits so your mother can take you home.'

'Don't talk to me like that!'

'Like what?'

'Like I'm a child. You're always ordering me around. What gives you the right?'

'Age and experience.'

'You mean arrogance,' I threw back. 'So you're just going to go back to fiddling around in your little turret room until you can't stand it any longer? Because if they're getting stronger, how long will it be until you're begging a brant to take you to Lharmell, just to make it all stop? And what about me? My people? They're freezing, Rodden. They're all going to die.'

'I know. But it's not your responsibility to deal with this.'

'How can you say that? They're *my* people'

'This problem is everyone's, not just Amentia's.'

'*Then why haven't you done anything?*' I was fighting to keep my voice down and the words came out in a growl.

'Because I'm not ready yet. The mines haven't been set up in Amentia and this is almost all the yelbar I have.'

'Listen to yourself! Making excuses. You're just scared.'

'You don't know anything about me,' he snarled.

I glared at him, breathing heavily. 'I want to help.'

'No.'

'Why not? You said yourself we're the only people who can come here without being poisoned to death.'

'You're royalty. You have a responsibility to your people.'

'Lilith's done enough duty for the both of us. Because of her, our people are not going to starve. But they could still freeze. I'm of more use to them here, where I can fight, than married to a rich man. In the end, what use will food be to them if they're frozen in the streets? Or turned into harmings?'

'We've got a long journey back. Surely we can argue about this at the palace.'

I picked up my bow. 'I don't want to go back.'

'What?' he exclaimed.

'This thing, this Turning. Is there one happening soon?'

'Yes, but –'

'And will the leader be there?'

He looked at me stonily. 'Zeraphina. No. It's far too dangerous.'

'Why? Because I'm a girl? I'm an excellent archer, you know that.'

'It's not enough,' he said. 'There will be hundreds of them. We have no supplies, nothing.'

'We have weapons and arrows. We could kill a brant if we need blood.'

He ran a hand through his hair.

'I can't go back without doing something,' I said, my voice tight in my throat. 'I can't. Even if we just go to one of these Turnings and watch, we might learn something.'

'There are people who love you, Zeraphina. People who care whether you live or die. I can't ask you to risk your life. Me, I have no one. I'm expendable.'

I reached out a hand and touched his leg. 'I care.' And I did. If he died or was Turned, no matter how irritating and frustrating he was, I would miss him. He was probably the first and last person in the world who was ever going to understand me, who knew what I was struggling with because he was struggling with the same thing.

He met my gaze. His eyes were less certain now. 'We might learn nothing. Do you really want to risk everything when the chance of failure is so high?'

'Truthfully, I want to go back to Amentia. Put my head in the sand. Shoot arrow after arrow and try to ignore the pain. But now that I know the truth, how can I?'

Rodden put his head in his hands. He sighed heavily. 'I can't believe I'm agreeing to this.'

I felt a flash of elation, and then a pang of alarm. We were going to do this. I'd just talked both of us into a suicide mission.

Rodden pointed a finger at me. 'I'm in charge. You do what I say and if at any point I say we're leaving, then we're leaving.'

'Yessir,' I said, with the same tone Hoggit used when taking orders.

'Then we'll go a little way in. Maybe not all the way to the tors, or the Turning, but as far as we can while it's still safe. Then we'll go back, and no arguing. Drink up.' He held out the flask to me.

I grimaced, but took a swig. It tasted even better that it did in my dreams. Better than anything I'd ever tasted in my life. As I drained the flask and licked my lips I felt a little guilty that I enjoyed it so much. I was taking to being a harming like a duck to water.

THIRTEEN

Rodden handed me one of the packs. 'We've each got a water skin, a small packet of food, two dozen arrows and a bow. Keep your hood up at all times. If we see anyone, we can pass as part-harmings if you keep your head down and your thoughts under control.'

'How do I do that?'

'Blinker them. Here, practise on Leap.' He picked up my cat and sat him on his lap. Leap purred and rubbed his cheek against Rodden's chest. He was such a sucker for attention. 'Ask him to do something with thought-pictures, like twitch his ears.'

I formed a thought-picture of Leap twitching his ears with my mind and sent it to him with something that I hoped seemed like 'please' tacked on the end.

Leap looked at me, wide-eyed, and his ears twitched. I laughed delightedly.

'That was very polite,' said Rodden. 'Almost made me want to twitch mine.'

'You heard me?'

'Yes, it was effective but unfocused, and far too loud. Try again, but make it just for Leap.'

I tried making the picture smaller and gave it a little nudge. Leap's ears twitched again.

'That's better. I still heard you but it was very faint. Now try, but before you send the pattern, put up a big wall all around your mind so the thought can't get through.'

I imagined the palace walls in Pergamia, steep and impenetrable. I built them up first, and then gave the thought-picture a little nudge towards Leap. He looked around in surprise, as if he'd heard something, but his ears didn't move.

'Good, but next time put a roof on your walls so the thoughts don't escape over the top. We should get going.'

I was surprised that Rodden knew with such accuracy what my wall had looked like. As I shouldered my pack, a ghastly thought occurred to me. 'You can't read my mind, can you?'

'No, of course not. I can just hear you when you let your thoughts go sparking off in all directions.

Especially when you're angry. And you're angry with me a lot, so I block that out. You're very keen to tell me in words just what you think of me so I don't need to hear it twice. And they,' he said, indicating Leap and Griffin, 'can hear you when you tell them how much you love them, which is pretty much every time you look at them.'

I had no idea my thoughts were so noisy. I remembered how, as I'd been getting ready for the ball, I'd been wondering if Rodden would be there. I hoped he hadn't heard me then. He would get entirely the wrong idea.

Rodden put his hood up and grinned at me from underneath it. The orange lamp-light made him look quite wicked. 'And what idea would that be? That you're a rotten show-off?'

I blanched. He'd just heard me then. I would have to be more careful.

'You needn't have worried,' he said, reaching over to pull my own hood up. 'I wouldn't have missed that dress for anything.'

I rolled my eyes. 'Move out, soldier.'

The sky was just beginning to lighten. I stood at the cave mouth, hooking my bow and arrows to the pack at easy grabbing distance. I usually liked dawn. It was a fresh, hopeful time of day, everything turning rosy and golden as the sun broke over the horizon. But in Lharmell, the dawn was sickly. The sun turned the clouds greenish and was doing very little to lighten the blackness of the dead forest. I shivered. The cloak was warm but while it kept the cold out it couldn't keep the other sort of goose-bumps from my skin: the sort caused by being totally spooked. At least at this time of day we wouldn't bump into any Lharmellins, but there might be harmings around. There were at least two about on that cold morning. Us.

Rodden emerged and looked around. 'Home sweet home, hey?'

'Don't even joke about that. Which way are we going?'

'You were headed in exactly the right direction when I found you yesterday: straight to the tors.'

'I thought I was heading for the ocean.'

We started walking. I was very glad to have a pair of good sturdy boots as it made the going infinitely easier.

'The tors act like a sort of homing beacon and they probably turned you around. If you pay attention to them, they can act like a compass. Right now I can feel us getting closer, like there's an invisible cord pulling us forwards. On the way back, you'll feel the cord lengthening, but reluctantly. It will always try to pull you back. But the good thing is you can navigate your way around the whole world without a compass, just by feeling where the tors are.'

I nodded. I'd felt that cord and the pain it could cause. But I'd also felt another. The one that had yanked me back the night I'd taken off on the brant. The one that had been connected to Rodden's agonised thought-pattern that had sounded like *No!* It had been almost as powerful as the cord that connected me to the tors.

Griffin flashed overhead, disappearing and reappearing among the trees. Rodden nodded to her. 'She'll keep an eye out. We're not likely to come across any Lharmellins during the day, but there could be harmings about. Leap's keeping watch, too.'

'How far is it?'

'You tell me.'

'You don't know?'

'Of course I do. But so do you. You have the same instincts as me, so work it out.'

I felt around a bit with my mind, searching for the cord. But Leap and Griffin kept getting in the way. Rodden's mind was completely closed; he wasn't giving anything away. Leap's mind was fuzzy and warm, his thoughts swarming like a cloud of midges as he took in sights, smells and sounds all at once. I wondered that he could concentrate on anything with all that thought-noise. Griffin was all about her eyes: her mind was clean and focused and razor sharp. I was getting just as much interference from her, though, because her thoughts were so directed.

'They'll never stop,' Rodden said. 'You have to learn to block them out when you need to.'

'Give me a break. This is all new to me,' I grumbled. I tried again, wiping everything *cat* and *eagle* from my mind. After a second I felt a faint tug, and fastened my mind onto the thread.

'That's *me*,' Rodden said, surprised.

'You were supposed to have your mind closed.'

'I did.'

'Well, close it some more.' I tried again. There it was, the white-blue cord, as cold as ice but strong as steel, pulling me onwards to the tors. I tested it, tugging back, feeling the distance between us.

'Got it?' asked Rodden.

'Yes. It's far, but . . .' I imagined the distance in paces, as if I was walking the cord like a tightrope. 'About a day-and-a-half's walk?'

Rodden nodded. 'About that.'

We walked in silence for a while. I wanted to ask Rodden why I could still pick up his thought-pattern when he had his mind closed, but he didn't seem to be in a talkative mood any more.

We rested when the sun was directly overhead, sitting on our packs to keep off the poisonous dirt. The clouds had begun to thin but there was still little warmth in the air.

'Eat the bread and cheese. It'll go stale soon anyway.'

I resisted the urge to snap that I would eat or drink what I pleased, but he must have heard me anyway as he muttered, 'Fine, do what you like.'

I ate because I was going to do it anyway. I just didn't want him to think I was doing it because of his say-so. When I'd finished I pushed the dirt around with the toe of my boot. 'What makes the forest so toxic?'

'There's a sort of acid rain that falls occasionally. The Lharmellins make it to keep the humans out. But the harmings and brants don't like it much either so they don't do it very often.' He glanced at the sky. The clouds had gathered again but they were pale and thin. 'We really don't want to get caught in an acid storm. It's a good thing everything is so toxic right now as it means they've probably just had one.'

Acid storms. What a charming bunch these Lharmellins were. 'How do you know so much about this place?' I asked. 'You said you'd been trained. What did you mean by that?'

'Nothing,' he said, stuffing the remains of his lunch back into his pack.

'Have you been here before?'

'No.'

'You said you weren't Pergamian. Where are you from?'

'I'm not in the mood to reminisce, Zeraphina.' He stood up, shouldering his pack.

The way was getting steeper now so I saved my breath for walking. Sometime in the mid-afternoon, craggy mountaintops rose behind the trees.

'The tors?' I asked.

Rodden nodded.

By twilight the trees had begun to thin and the ground was rocky with lots of boulders and loose stones scattered around, scree from the mountains. We found a sort of natural dolmen, a large flat rock being supported by two others that formed a shelter.

Rodden gave it a sharp kick. 'It's solid,' he pronounced.

'And you determined this how?' I asked, walking

around the structure. If it collapsed in the night we would be squashed like bugs. I leaned heavily against it in several places, testing its soundness.

'I said it's fine.'

'Do you want to fight about it or can I just get on with it?' I snapped. I watched Rodden throw his pack under the dolmen and slump against it, his eyes closed. He looked bone tired.

I crawled in after him. 'Have you slept since the ball?'

He kept his eyes closed and shook his head.

'Oh.' He stayed silent, and I sensed the inadequacy of the 'oh'. Because it would gall me, and because he would probably throw it back in my face, I was reluctant to express any gratitude. But I had to. 'Thank you,' I said. 'For coming to find me. I thought I was going to die.'

'Any time,' he mumbled.

Leap walked the length of my legs and curled up between us, instantly falling asleep.

Talking about the ball made me think of Renata and Lilith for the first time all day. I missed them with a force that surprised me. But bossy and interfering as she was, Renata always had my best interests at heart. And I would give anything to hear Lilith call me Fina again. I was even more surprised to find that I was homesick for Amentia and our cold, dreary castle.

I sighed heavily. 'I'll keep first watch,' I offered.

'No need. Griffin's dozing in a tree out there. She'll wake us if something happens.'

I made my pack into a makeshift pillow and lay down. The ground was horribly hard and cold, but it was better than being on my feet. Rodden looked like he was already asleep. His face was roughened by stubble, but as he wasn't frowning for the moment he looked almost agreeable.

I wasn't sleepy just yet so I examined the thought-threads in my mind. There was Leap's, vibrating with purrs and warmth. Griffin's was sharp and alert. The tor-line was thick and strong now that we were so close. But I pushed these three aside, searching for another. There it was, humming away quietly: the thread between me and the man sleeping beside me. I brushed it with my mind, very softly. He noticed and clamped down on it immediately, severing our connection.

'Go to sleep.'

'Sorry,' I whispered back.

'Hmph. Always poking your nose in . . .'

After the initial coven of Lharmellins I'd stumbled into we'd been blood-sucking-monster-free – apart from ourselves of course. We couldn't continue to be so lucky, especially not this close to the tors.

Between them, Griffin and Leap woke us four times that night.

I would like to say that the first occasion was the worst. But it wasn't. Each time a blazing, anxious *wake up!* thought-pattern shocked me out of consciousness I think I died a little inside.

When the first alarm came, I realised I'd stupidly left my bow and arrows hooked to my pack and I couldn't get to them without dragging them out from underneath everything. Not only would it be far too noisy to do so, it wasn't exactly the best place to store delicate weaponry. I sent a miserable *can't* to Rodden when he asked me what the hell I was playing at and could I get my weapon out already? He had his bow trained on the blackness and replied with an image of a wall, telling me to block my thoughts. I concentrated on doing so while I searched the landscape for tell-tale bluish glows and listening for the clicks that would announce a pack of Lharmellins on the hunt. I could barely see a thing, and the only sounds were the crunch of stones underfoot, far off. It was a decidedly non-Lharmellin sound.

Eventually I heard Rodden un-notch his arrow. 'Harmings,' he whispered. 'Just a handful and Griffin says they've gone. Where's your weapon?'

'Under my pack.'

'Why?'

'Because I left it there,' I hissed. I had already been chastising myself enough.

'Well, get it out now.'

'I *am*.'

'Don't shoot anything unless we're spotted. We don't want to draw attention to our presence here. We want them to think that after killing those Lharmellins we left or died in the poisonous forest, not that we travelled closer to the tors.'

'We should have decided this before we went to sleep,' I grumbled.

'I already did. I thought it was obvious, but apparently not to someone who can't keep her weapon handy.'

I slapped my bow down at easy grabbing distance and turned my back to him.

'And put a lid on all those irritated thoughts. Anything could hear you.'

I thought about asking Leap to bite his hand but decided that while it was tempting, it was also rather unethical.

The second time we were woken I was up and aiming before Rodden had his eyes open – probably because I had been fuming too much to sleep. I heard the dull thud of footsteps against hard-packed earth, and then a skittering of stones. It had to be harmings again as Lharmellins didn't technically walk. There seemed to be about a dozen of them and they were heading up the mountain. The sounds grew fainter and we both relaxed, easing ourselves back down without a word.

The third and fourth times were much the same: footsteps in the dark. 'We must be near a mountain pass,' Rodden said softly as the fourth group faded away.

'Do you think they're looking for us?'

'It's hard to say.'

I remembered what he'd said about acid storms. It seemed a rather too effective way of clearing the forest of unwanted guests. I just hoped there were too many harmings about to make it worth the Lharmellins' while.

Rodden shook me awake at first light. This was my third morning in Lharmell, and it was starting to show. My hair was a tangled mess, I was grimy and I was starting to stink. Rodden was in much the same condition. I poured the tiniest amount of water on a rag I'd saved from my petticoat and wiped it over my face and neck. It refreshed me a little despite the fractured night's sleep.

Griffin had been on a morning hunt and to my surprise she was butchering a large rat in a tree. Leap was sitting nearby, and I saw her drop down the hindquarters for him. Leap snatched it up and scurried off with his prize.

Rodden drained the flask and shouldered his pack. 'There's life nearby. We should try to hunt.' He turned to me. 'Or have you had enough? Ready to go home perhaps?'

I shouldered my pack. 'You can go. I'm fine.'

His eyebrows rose as if in surprise, but he quickly dropped the expression.

Together we looked to the mountains rising steeply ahead of us.

'The tors surround a circular valley, which is what we're aiming for,' Rodden said. 'Judging from last night's foot-traffic there must be a pass very near here,' he continued. 'What do you reckon, over there?'

I looked at where he was pointing. There was a crease in the ranges where two peaks met. It wasn't too high up, but the going looked steep. I shook my head. 'There must be an easier way to get in. Did the harmings leave any tracks?'

We looked around us at the scree but the jumbled stones were giving nothing away.

I scanned the mountains again. 'There,' I said. 'Where those trees extend up the mountain a bit. Right above that, it looks like a pass.'

'That's even higher than the other one.'

'But it's less steep.'

Rodden considered this, and then nodded. 'All right, then.'

What, no argument?

Rodden notched an arrow. 'Keep your eyes peeled for rats. They don't taste as nice as rabbits, but they'll do. If we can shoot a couple it will save us slaughtering a brant, which might bring us unwanted attention.'

The rocky ground was tricky to clamber over. As the gradient increased, so did the amount of slipping and sliding we did over the loose stones. I was grateful for my gloves, as they meant my hands weren't torn to ribbons. Leap was light and agile enough to bound up ahead of us. Griffin flew ahead and then glowered down at our pathetic progress.

'This can't be the right way,' Rodden muttered. 'I can't believe the harmings do this all the time.'

'Maybe that's a good thing,' I panted. 'We don't want to go barrelling in their front door.'

'What if there's only one entrance and we're just wasting time?'

'Call a brant down then. We'll fly in.'

'Too conspicuous.'

Just then the stones beneath my feet gave way. Rodden snatched at my hand, missed, and I could do nothing but slide painfully down the mountainside on my right leg. A sharp rock sliced into my calf. I doubled up in pain and pressed my hands over the wound, biting my cheek so I didn't cry out.

Rodden came scrambling down after me. 'Are you okay?'

I didn't bother to respond to such an inane question.

'Here, let me see,' he said, prising my fingers off my leg. Blood had started to soak my trousers. I looked at the gash. It was about a foot long, but I couldn't see how deep. Rodden poked at it with his fingers and the pain was intense.

'Stop touching it!' I gasped.

'I have to check it. I think you're okay. It's just a bad scratch.' He pulled some clean white cloth out of his pack and began tearing it into strips. 'I don't like all this blood everywhere,' he muttered.

'There's a first.'

He gave me a wry look. 'I mean it could be dangerous. They'll know we came this way.'

'Part-harmings might come this way all the time.'

'Yes, but what happens when a good little convert with a big cut doesn't turn itself in? They'll know it's us.' He bound my leg up tightly and sat back on his heels. 'Maybe it's time we called down a brant and went home.'

'No. We've come this far already.'

'Can you go any further? I doubt you can even walk.'

'I can,' I insisted. I stood up and tested my leg. It hurt like hell, but I was determined. I looked up at the pass. 'I'll make a deal with you,' I said. 'If I can't reach that pass, or if it turns out to be blocked somehow, we'll get a brant home.'

Rodden gave me a long look. Again, I was expecting an argument but he just nodded.

This time he went first, testing the ground before he put his foot down. While we were going over the rockier parts he kept a hold of my hand. I was preoccupied with the pain in my leg and the worry that I was leaving a blood trail, so it came as a surprise to me when my feet landed on dirt as well as stone and the ground levelled out.

Rodden looked down. 'No footprints. This isn't the pass that was used last night.'

I found a rock and slumped onto it, not bothering to remove my pack.

'How's the leg?'

I looked at him through half-closed eyes. 'A real picnic.'

He crouched down beside me and notched up an arrow.

'Are we in danger?'

'No,' he whispered. 'I see a rat.' He drew back and fired, then jumped up so I guessed that he must have found his mark. I sat dozing in the afternoon sunlight, the rough night catching up with me. I was just imagining having a long, hot bath in my room in Pergamia when something landed in my lap. My eyes snapped open to see an enormous dead rat. It was all I could do not to start shrieking. I wasn't particularly frightened of rats but I was on edge and a dead, bloodied creature falling out of the sky was unsettling at the best of times.

'All yours,' Rodden said graciously.

I hadn't yet worked up the nerve to touch it. The arrow had pierced the thing's rib-cage, but it wasn't the wound that was appalling me the most. It was the rat's long, hairless, floppy tail. 'I think I'm going to be sick. Can't you put the blood in a flask or something?'

'Just hurry up and suck on the wound before it clots. It'll help your cut heal faster.'

I looked at the rat again. I didn't want to touch it, let alone put my mouth on it.

Leap ate them all the time, I reasoned. So did Griffin. If it was good enough for them . . .

I raised the furry body to my mouth, fighting down my gag reflex. Once I got going it wasn't too bad. There wasn't much blood in it, but I found what little I drank made my leg throb a bit less. I threw the carcass to Leap, who was far more excited about it than I was. I wiped my hand across my mouth, trying to rid myself of the feel of its fur. I shuddered and said, as gratefully as I could manage, 'Thank you.'

Rodden bowed. 'My pleasure, Your Highness,' he said in his best courtly voice.

'You toad,' I said. 'You think this is funny?'

He grinned. 'Just a little. The high and mighty Princess Zeraphina just ate rat.'

I narrowed my eyes at him. 'You will regret this.' My threat wasn't as convincing as I would have liked as a moment later I had to ask him to help me up.

We approached the pass with some trepidation.

'Do you think they have guards?' I whispered.

'Difficult to say, but I think not. Those woods keep the humans away, and I doubt they'd consider a threat from their own kind. As far as I know, we're the first harming rebels.'

Rebels. I liked the sound of that.

Just to be sure, we asked Griffin to scout ahead for us. She flew into the pass, disappeared for about two minutes and then flew back. She sent a thought-picture to us, showing a narrow but acceptable path through the mountains, free from harmings and Lharmellins.

Rodden turned to me. 'So this is it. The point of no return.'

'I thought I passed that three days ago.'

'Are you sure you can do this?'

I tested my leg. It still hurt, but I was limping less and I thought I could even run if I needed to. 'Yes.'

'From this point on, I'm a harming bringing you to the fold. I can pass for a full harming but I don't think you can. Keep your head down, your hood up and your mind closed. If we come across other harmings, which we likely will, don't lose your nerve. Let me do the talking. And tell Leap and Griffin they have to keep out of sight.'

It was dark between the mountains and sheer walls rose on both sides. Any stone that we kicked by accident made a lot of racket, the noise amplified by echoes. Neither of us spoke, though I desperately wanted to ask Rodden what he thought was on the other side. I dared not do it by thought-patterns, either, in case everything on the mountain heard me.

A long, thin shriek made me jump three feet in the air. Leap flattened himself against the ground.

'Brant chick,' Rodden said. 'There's a nest right above us.'

Sure enough, a ball of sharp black twigs was wedged high up in a crevice. A bald, pink chick glared down at us with beady eyes.

It was dusk when we emerged on the other side. The panoramic view of curving mountains on all sides was breathtaking. They were bluish and windswept and totally barren. The far side must have been five miles away. I looked down into the bowl-shaped valley but all I could see was darkness. The sky had cleared and the sun had prematurely set over the rim of mountains. A little way below us there was some greenery and I hoped there was a forest further down. I felt more at home in the cover of living trees.

'It's a huge volcanic crater,' Rodden said. 'These mountains are made from basalt and black glass. Spewed out of the earth, in other words.'

'So we're teetering on the brink of something dangerous?' I asked.

'You could say that.'

'Do you have a plan?'

'We save humanity from slavery and death.'

'Could you be more specific?'

'Not right now, no.'

We descended into the darkness. There was indeed a forest in the valley, and to my utter delight, a stream.

'It's a mineral spring, coming up out of the mountains. It looks safe to drink.'

'I don't want to drink, I want to wash. Now go away.'

He folded his arms. 'I don't know if it's safe to leave you alone.'

'I'm not asking you to go out of earshot. Just go sit behind a tree.'

He looked around, scanning the forest. 'Fine. Keep your leg dry.'

The water wasn't deep enough to bathe, but I gave myself a pretty good scrub with a rag. Even after all this time I was still washing gold powder off my shoulders. I dearly wanted some soap but Rodden hadn't thought to bring any, so all I could do was wash the dust from my hair and tie it back with another rag. By the time I was done I was shivering but pleasantly refreshed, even inside my filthy clothes.

Rodden came back with a dead brant chick and another rat. 'The choice is yours, my lady. I don't normally drink blood in the evenings, as it keeps you awake, but tonight is different.'

'Why.'

'We're not sleeping tonight.'

I sighed. 'Give me the chick then.' Neither of the dead animals appealed to me, but if I had to suck rat, so did he. We were finishing off our dinner when we saw cloaked figures approaching. I hastily pulled my hood up and put a wall around my mind. Leap and Griffin sank into the shadows.

Rodden stood, moving towards the party and deliberately putting himself between them and me. He raised his hand in greeting. In the other the rat still dangled by its tail.

'Glory to Lharmell,' I heard one the figures at the front say.

'Glory to Lharmell,' Rodden repeated. 'An impressive flock.'

'Yes,' replied the harming, pride in his voice. 'Six converts.'

'I have but one,' Rodden replied, sounding rather disappointed.

I felt something like black tentacles probing at my mind. It was the harming. He didn't get far as I'd sealed my mind like a vice.

'She's a dim creature,' observed the harming.

'Indeed she is,' Rodden replied.

I resisted the urge to scowl. I could see the other 'converts' shuffling nervously, as if they were anxious to get going.

'There is a Turning tonight,' said the harming.

The others broke into excited whispers. 'A Turning. A Turning,' they said to each other.

I made myself echo their childish tone. 'A Turning.'

'We shall see you there,' replied Rodden. 'Praise for blood.'

'Praise for blood,' replied the harming, and he and his flock moved off into the trees.

Rodden walked back, throwing the rat into the bushes. He grinned at me. 'Good work with the dim creature act. Your mind-blocking is getting better.'

'How did you know to say "praise for blood" instead of just "goodbye"?' I asked suspiciously. 'I thought you hadn't been here before.'

Rodden sat down beside me. 'All right. You got me. The past three days have been an elaborate ruse to lull you into a false sense of security. Rescuing you. Killing six Lharmellins. Teaching you to outwit other harmings. Just to see the look on your face when I hand you over. I can't wait.'

I sniffed. 'I wouldn't put it past you.'

'I told you, I've been trained.'

'Yes, but you didn't say how.'

'Now is hardly the time. We have a Turning to attend.'

'And what's that?'

'Exactly what it sounds like. Here's a hint: don't drink anything.'

We hid our packs under some bushes and our weapons under our cloaks next to our bodies. I bid Leap and Griffin goodbye, urging them to stay out of sight.

And then, trying not to feel like a lamb to the slaughter, I let Rodden lead me to the Turning.

FOURTEEN

From beneath my hood I watched the harmings arrive. There were hundreds of them, trickling down to the very base of the valley. They gathered in the clearing as the last rays of the sun disappeared from the sky. The Evening Star appeared, and then as the sky darkened from azure to sapphire, a thousand more emerged above the natural enclosure of the mountains. The moon rose, bloated and yellow, climbing above the rim of the tors like a night-god's eye to witness the events below. Tremors of excitement ran through the crowd. Brants swirled overhead. There was no sign of the Lharmellins yet, but we could feel them coming.

It took all my concentration to keep my thoughts to myself and others' out. Strange and hideous thought-patterns exploded in my head before fading rapidly. They were violent and bloodied contemplations and I hoped I wasn't reliving someone's horrific deeds. I squeezed my eyes shut, willing the images to stop.

Rodden took my gloved hand and squeezed it gently, and I experienced a ripple of cool and calm flow up my arm. I felt the thread between us, thrumming like a bow-string.

A hush fell over the crowd. Rodden kept a firm grip on my hand as four Lharmellins appeared atop the large flat rock at the other end of the clearing.

The Lharmellins on the rock began to sing. The crowd moaned and we were thrust forward by a press of bodies. I could make out what sounded like a strange language, but the four seemed to be speaking different words at once, garbling the foreign tongue. The effect was eerie, yet beautiful. The horde of harmings was enraptured, Turned and un-Turned alike, maniacal grins on their faces.

A fifth Lharmellin appeared atop the rock. The crowd sobbed with love for the creature, their hands reaching to it as if they were drowning. This Lharmellin wore a black robe like the others, but it was stitched with strange patterns that glowed ice-blue like its eyes. The hood fell back, revealing its face. The thing was hairless and a mass of puffy blue veins. Its mouth was just as it appeared in my book: lipless, baring dozens of needle-like teeth. It glared out at the crowd, a look of fierce joy in its expression. Gloating at the frenzy of the harmings below.

It raised its arms, and its voice joined the others in song, coiling its notes through the others', bringing the chorus to a crescendo of madness. I was thrust against my neighbours by the jostling harmings, pinned front and back by bodies. I fought to keep a grip on Rodden's hand.

There was no doubt in my mind that we beheld the leader. Killing it was our goal tonight. I felt Rodden's agreement surge along our connecting thread. With my free hand I fingered an arrow but in the crowd there was no room to draw a bow. And if we did kill it, right there in front of everyone, what would the harmings do to us?

The leader turned to its neighbour on the rock, raised its claw-like fingers and ripped out the Lharmellin's throat while it was mid-song. Unperturbed, the others kept up their song. Dark blood sprayed over the harmings, and the mob went wild. They screamed for blood. They threw their heads back and bayed at the moon. I was shoved forward and I lost my grip on Rodden. The second our hands parted the blood-hunger bloomed in my chest. I was whipped into a frenzy by the potent smell of Lharmellin blood and I screamed with the rest of them. I scrabbled at those in front of me, trying to pull them out of my way. I had to get to the dying Lharmellin, the blood that pumped from its throat.

The harmings tried to climb the rock, reaching with desperate arms. The leader shredded the throat of another Lharmellin with its sharp nails and threw it into the mob. It was still alive, its singing garbled by blood. Harmings leapt for the fallen creature. The bodies in front of me parted and I leapt forwards. I was faster than the others and was at the front first. There were other harmings lapping at the rock where the blood flowed down and still others trying to scale the face of it. I felt hands grab my cloak and try to pull me away. I smashed my elbow into another harming's nose and she howled with pain.

Mine, a voice snarled in my head. My voice, wild like a starving animal's.

I worked my way around the rock, searching for a way to scale it. Rodden, still trapped in the mob, was letting off a frantic *NONONONONO* and it was scrambling my concentration. I threw a furious *STOP!* at him and felt him reel backwards. My fingers found purchase on the rock and I hauled myself up, kicking away the hands of those who tried to follow me. I reached the top and stood, and found myself face-to-face with the Lharmellin in the glowing robe.

The clamour from the mob died away until all I could hear was the Lharmellins' singing. I felt such bittersweet pain, such joy. Tears ran down my face. The creature grinned, gloating over the utter supplication in my eyes. I fell to my knees before it.

Something was trying to yank me from the rock but I could feel no hands on my body, only a flaming pain in my chest. It burned, tongues of heat licking at my insides, making me scream. The dead Lharmellin, blood still pouring from its throat and down the boulder, was just a few feet away. The smell was intoxicating, but I could still feel a bombardment of near-hysterical thought-pictures and an incessant pulling at my insides, making me writhe in pain.

I wished it would *stop*.

I would make it stop. It was *him*. I would stop him, I would kill him. I would crunch his bones with my bare hands and lap at the rivers of blood that would run down my arms.

The pain stopped abruptly.

My arms.

With a swift movement I shook down the arrows that I'd slipped into my sleeves. There was no time for my bow, and no space to draw. My eyes were blurred with tears.

I will be free.

Break the skin, let the poison in.

Break the skin.

A face flashed before me, angered, familiar, then the Lharmellin's. My eyes cleared and I saw my love standing before me. *My love.* Though it shredded my heart I knew what I had to do to make it *stop*.

I gripped the shafts of the arrows and thrust upwards with all the strength in my arms, plunging the points into the leader's belly. Brackish blood flowed over my fingers.

The Lharmellin's grin faltered and it looked to its stomach with something like surprise. It opened its mouth to shriek, its clawed hands rising to strike me. I pressed the shafts deeper, up into its ribcage, feeling the crackle of bone and gristle. The icy light in the Lharmellin's eyes turned a sickly orange as the yelbar coursed through its system. I waited for the creature's dying revenge, the claws to swipe at my throat. But its flesh began to blacken and smoke, and then its body disintegrated inside its robe.

I felt sweet release, the poisonous frenzy ebbing away with the blood that ran like venomous rivers down my arms. There was a tug on my insides, the familiar thrum of the tall man's thread, he of the arrows and the watchful eyes, whispering my name over and over in fury and relief.

The crowd staggered, stared, and then let rip with a mighty roar of outrage. The remaining two Lharmellins turned on me with a shriek and I fumbled for another arrow. Then they were shrieking in pain, arrows sprouting from their chests and I knew Rodden had found the space to fire.

I leapt off the back of the rock, hit the ground running and pelted away with all the strength I had in my legs. I cast a desperate thought for Leap and Griffin to follow me, hoping the harmings wouldn't hear me.

I was headed straight into the unknown, away from Rodden and the mountain pass, perhaps directly into the path of more Lharmellins. I had to get away from the baying mob behind me. They wanted my blood. They wanted to rip the flesh from my bones. I could hear them wanting it, screaming for it.

As I ran my eyes scanned the forest. It was thick, which gave me cover, but it also made it difficult to negotiate. One slip-up and they would be on me. I'd had a small head-start while the harmings were still reeling, but they were gaining on me now. The tors were lit up by the full moon and I made them my aim.

Griffin, a pass! I called to her. *Find a pass.* I felt her wheel away to the mountains. I desperately wanted to send a thought-pattern to Rodden but I didn't trust myself to cast it with accuracy. He was within the crowd of harmings and if I sent anything I might blanket the lot with my whereabouts. I hoped that he would locate Leap, who was making a beeline for me.

Griffin flashed a thought-picture to me: it was an unguarded pass to the north-west, roughly the direction I was headed, but miles off. I would never make it on foot. My lungs were burning with the need for air. The frenzied harmings would overtake me before long. I looked to the sky. Brants were flapping erratically overhead, unsettled by the commotion below. I had ten arrows, the quiver tucked inside my robe with my bow. There was a break in the trees up ahead and I made for it, hurling a command at the closest brant. I notched an arrow and aimed as the enormous bird descended, ready for anything that might be on its back.

The wind whipped up, and on it I heard the voices of the Lharmellins, their singing frantic now and purposeful. How could they sing at a time like this?

A harming broke through the trees, saw me and screamed in anger. He was un-Turned, practically human. Except for his face which was contorted into a mask of rage and frustrated blood-lust. I re-aimed and loosed the arrow, striking the thing through its neck. It crumpled to the ground. I hoped I had killed before it could summon any others.

I heard a rumbling overhead. Great banks of greenish clouds were appearing over the tors. Lightning flashed. The brant overhead baulked and tried to fly away but I grabbed it with my mind and yanked it down. It was riderless. I held it in place and searched around me for Leap.

Where were the harmings? They should have caught up with me by now.

The moon disappeared, obliterated by the encroaching clouds, and I realised why the harmings had scattered: the Lharmellins were calling down an acid storm. Fear shot through me. There was no cover anywhere near me, and where was Rodden?

Leap burst out of a bush and I snatched him up. I climbed onto the brant's back, settled my cat in front of me and flung an *up* command at the bird. As we rose into the air I sent frantic thought-patterns to Rodden, not caring now what might hear me. The clouds above the valley were thickening. I couldn't tell how long until the acid started to rain down on us, but it wouldn't be long.

I guided the brant back to where the Turning had been, scanning the ground with my eyes and mind. A hiss from Leap made my head snap up. A brant being ridden by a Lharmellin was bearing down on us, talons first. I brought up my bow, wavering between the brant and the rider for an instant, and then shot the bird in the neck. As I fumbled for another arrow the raptor tipped off balance and tumbled to the ground, taking the Lharmellin with it.

The sky cleared of brants. The storm was going to break at any moment. I hollered Rodden's name with thought-patterns before remembering the cord between us. I wiped the other threads from my mind, found his and yanked with all my might. There! I grasped the reins as we dove through the trees. The brant struck the ground at speed and I tumbled off. The impact winded me but I struggled up, bow drawn. Rodden was fighting off a group of harmings, using his bow as a staff. I had eight arrows left and used four to pick the harmings off before they knew I was there. A remaining three glanced at the sky and sprinted off.

Rodden spotted me and ran over. 'Acid storm,' he gasped. 'Make for the dolmen.'

We climbed onto the brant. It was getting stroppy having to carry two people and a cat, and the thunder overhead was unsettling it. It flapped its wings, rising up on the tips of its talons to shake us off. I sent an urgent *flee* picture to it that carried all my terror of the approaching storm. It got the message and shot into the air, fear overcoming its stubbornness. To Griffin I cast a picture of the dolmen. We would have to fly through the pass we had traversed earlier. It would take too long to fly over the tors. I prayed the brant would be able to navigate the narrow space in the agitated state it was in.

The night had grown dark and the tors rushed towards us out of nowhere. The brant dipped a wing towards the ground, flying at an angle to narrow its broad span. Its wingtips skimmed the parallel rock faces as we hurtled through at break-neck speed. The wind whistled in my ears. Rodden tugged my hood firmly over my head and reached his arms around me to grip the saddle. I folded Leap into my cloak and cast about for Griffin. She was behind us, but I couldn't tell how far. As we burst out of the pass the first drops of rain began to fall and I heard them sizzle on my cloak. I steered the brant down the tors, hoping that I was aiming for the dolmen. A lightning bolt lit up the sky brighter than day and I spotted it.

The brant screamed and shook its head frantic-ally. It had acid in its eyes. I plunged the bird into the ground and we skidded over the scree, coming to a halt about ten yards from the shelter. I half-fell, half-dismounted, felt Rodden haul me up by my arms and we stumbled over the uneven ground. Spots of acid fell on the backs of my hands and they burned like fire. We flung ourselves under the dolmen as the rain began to beat down.

'Griffin!' I screamed her name with my mind and my mouth. She'd been right behind us, I was sure of it. I waited for her to come hurtling out of the sky. She didn't. Outside, the brant was caught in the storm. It was screaming in pain, desperately flapping its wings. One looked to be broken. The rain began to strip the feathers from its body, the flesh beneath turning an angry red.

I turned to Rodden. 'You said the acid was only poisonous to humans.'

'After it's fallen, yes. Apparently not before.'

I gripped his arms. 'Then Griffin's out in it

somewhere. Where is she? I can't find her. I can't hear her.'

Rodden looked out into the night, searching for the eagle. He shook his head. 'The rain's throwing up too much interference. I can't trace her. She'll have found shelter, don't worry.' He kept a grip on my arm, as if worried that I was going to go back out in the storm to look for her.

I bit my lip hard, feeling tears begin to brim in my eyes. It could be the interference from the rain. Or she could be dead, stripped and burning in the storm. 'I should have warned her earlier. I sent her miles off to the north-west, looking for a pass. There was no way she was going to make it back here in time.' I looked down at Leap, checking for burns. He was unharmed, but his eyes were large and terrified.

'It's all right,' said Rodden. 'As soon as the storm stops we'll find her.'

I slumped against rock and closed my eyes. There was nothing to do except listen to the hiss of the rain and the screams of the dying brant.

———

The rain eased just before dawn. I had fallen into a fitful doze a few hours earlier, fatigue finally overcoming me.

I awoke to an alien world. Everything had either been bleached white or burnt black. The brant was a wreck of twisted, smoking bones. It looked too much like the fears I held for Griffin and I felt my stomach twist with nausea. I was about to loose a mental yell to her when Rodden stopped me.

'Let me do it. We want the Lharmellins to think we're dead. You're too upset to channel your thoughts.'

I reluctantly put my wall back up and scanned the sky with my eyes. Before Rodden could begin I saw a speck with beating wings come hurtling off the tors.

'There!' I cried. It was Griffin. I gave a triumphant, ear-splitting whistle and raised my wrist to her. She dived for us, pulled up and settled on my arm, making a clicking noise in her throat and ruffling her feathers. She was just as upset as I had been. I checked her over, but there wasn't a mark on her. Amazed, I asked her where she'd been. She showed me an image of the brant nest we had passed going into the mountain. She'd spent the night in the nest with the chick. I laughed with delight. 'Did you get that?' I asked Rodden.

'Loud and clear. Clever girl.'

He didn't seem as happy about Griffin's safety as I was. 'What's wrong?'

'How many arrows do you have?' he asked.

I checked my quiver. 'Four.'

'I have none and I lost my bow.'

'Then let's call a brant and get out of here.'

Rodden shook his head. 'It's too dangerous. They'll have a tight watch on them now they know we can control them. If we call one down we'll bring a whole army of harmings down on our heads too.'

'But there's no other way to get home. Unless we walk.'

'We have no supplies. There's nothing to hunt. Everything will have been killed by the acid storm. We don't have our packs so we have no water, either. We won't make it.'

'Then what? We need to get out of here.'

Rodden clenched his jaw and looked back at the tors.

'No,' I said. 'No way. I'm not going back in there. You heard them, they want to kill us. We'll call a brant.'

'It's too dangerous to do from here. If we get closer, they might not notice until it's too late. The Lharmellins won't be active right now, so there'll just be harmings on guard. Plus, they'll be disorganised. They have a whole valley full of frustrated part-harmings clamouring for Lharmellin blood.'

I considered this. Every fibre of my being was adamant that I didn't want to go back in there. But he was right. It was our only chance to get home. I sighed. 'Let's get going then.'

It was easier to scale the tors without our packs, though it was thirsty work. We had no food, no water and no blood. Griffin scouted ahead, flying back to us before sending any thought-pictures to keep our mind activity to a minimum. For the moment, the pass was clear. It would have been safer to find another entrance but we didn't have the time. We had to get a brant by nightfall before the Lharmellins could regroup and begin their hunt. I thought of the blue flashes among the trees, the clicking noises they made as they closed in on their prey. To be hunted in that way – the idea was terrifying. This time going in, there was no joking, no laughs. Our mouths were set in grim lines.

'You could have warned me,' Rodden said as we climbed, his voice tight with anger. 'At the Turning. I thought you were going to become one of them right before my eyes.'

'There wasn't time,' I muttered. I remembered the urge to kill, my confusion. The truth was I hadn't been sure what I was about to do. Someone had to die, and I was sick at the thought that I might have turned on Rodden, or even myself.

'I felt you hating me,' he said, his voice flat, colourless. 'I felt you wanting to kill me.'

I shook my head, unable to speak. I concentrated on putting one foot in front of the other.

'I felt you wanting to kill yourself.' His voice came from behind me.

I felt tears burn my eyes, as if they were made of acid. I was too tired to hold them back and they left searing trails down my face. The ground blurred in front of me and I had to stop or risk my footing. I swiped at my face, angry that a few drops of salt-water had hobbled me.

'Don't,' I said. 'I couldn't help it.'

I had hated him, loathed him, wanted to kill him, and he had heard it all.

He cursed, and caught my arm and turned me. 'I know,' he said. 'I'm sorry. Don't cry, I'm an idiot.'

I fumbled for a piece of sleeve that wasn't filthy so I could wipe my face.

With a moderately clean corner of his cloak he dabbed at my tears. I closed my eyes, avoiding his gaze.

'He of the arrows and the watchful eyes,' he murmured.

I opened my eyes in surprise, and he was smiling at me.

'You were only gone a few seconds, and that was your first thought when you came out of the frenzy. Do you remember?'

'I'd forgotten your name,' I said thickly.

He ran his eyes over my tear-stained face. 'I have to say, you were rather magnificent up there. Scary as hell, too. I think I was pulling at you so hard it was no wonder you wanted to kill me. It must have hurt.'

'It hurt,' I agreed. 'It hurt a lot. But I think it kept me on this side of sanity, so . . .' The words felt strange and inadequate in my mouth, dwarfed by the mountainside, the sheer size of the sky. '. . . thank you.'

His hand was still on my sleeve, which was spotted with holes from the acid rain. The air about us crackled with tension. He was looking at me the way he had in the ballroom, but this time there truly wasn't another soul around.

After three seconds had dragged by, I punched him on the shoulder. 'And don't be such a bully, or you'll make me cry again.'

———

We reached the pass. Griffin gave the all-clear and we started through. I felt sick with worry. It was all wrong, going back into a place where everything wanted us dead. But Rodden was right – we didn't have a great deal of choice. We would soon be hunted down or die of exposure if we stayed in the forest. I tried to comfort myself with all the things I was going to do when I got back to the palace. It would be before nightfall. We would get home by moonrise tonight, or we would die here.

'A bath,' I whispered to Rodden. 'That's the first thing I'm going to do when I get back to Pergamia: have a bath. I'll probably need ten baths to soak all this grime off me.'

He nodded. 'I'm going to shave.' He scratched his chin. 'And then I'm going to burn these clothes.'

'Burn mine, too. But not the boots. I quite like the boots.'

We approached the entrance to the valley with caution. The morning light showed that the valley had been stripped of greenery. All the trees were blackened and bare. The acid had killed everything. Nothing moved on the ground or in the sky. I realised how much of a miracle it was that we were still alive.

'Where will the brants be? They're not all dead, are they?'

Rodden shook his head. 'No, they would never

risk that. There must be an overhang or a cave somewhere. We could go looking for them, but it's too dangerous. We'll just have to wait and watch the sky. They'll have to feed their chicks soon. There'll be undisturbed land somewhere for them.'

'That nest in the pass. We could stake it out.'

'We could. It's risky, though. There are only two exits and they could be so easily blocked off.'

'What if I watch the inside entrance, you watch the outside entrance and Griffin watches the nest? Leap can be our go-between.'

'All right, but let me take the inside entrance.'

'Because it's more dangerous?'

'Yes.'

'But I have the bow and arrows.'

'Give them to me then.'

'I'm a better shot and you know it. Everyone in Xallentaria knows it.'

'By the tiniest fraction of an inch! It barely counts.'

'If the wind gets up and you don't correct for it properly . . .'

'Oh, shut up. Fine, take the inside entrance. Keep Leap walking between us. The pass is only five hundred yards long so he shouldn't be absent for more than fifteen minutes at a time. If he's gone longer than that, come running. Tell Griffin to alert us as soon as the brant comes back.'

We took our stations. Leap sat with me for a few minutes before turning and pacing to Rodden at the other end of the pass. I was glad he had slept in the dolmen the previous night as he might have to keep the walking up all day. I tested my bowstring and notched up an arrow. I was crouched behind a rock but I had a clear view of the valley below.

I began to see the holes in our plan. Once the brant came back to its nest, how were we going to coax it down without using thought-pictures? And what if the chick's parent was the one that had died in the storm last night? We could be waiting forever for a bird that was never going to turn up.

My eyes grew tired from staring at the landscape, but I couldn't afford to let up. Leap reappeared and disappeared six, seven, then eight times. He carried nothing from Rodden in his mind except a picture of him, exhausted but vigilant, at the mouth of the pass.

After another three circuits by Leap, I heard the flap of wings overhead. The brant was descending from directly above the pass, its wings beating awkwardly in the cramped space. I waited for it to settle on its nest before I crouched low and ran along the path towards Rodden and Leap. We met in the middle, twenty yards from the nest.

'Now what do we do?' I hissed. 'It's too far up to get to.'

Rodden stared up at the nest, shielding his eyes against the strip of bright sky above. Then he cursed.

'What?' I whispered.

'They've taken off its saddle and bridle.'

I looked. He was right. 'Can we still ride it?'

He seemed doubtful. 'Maybe. If we upset it, though, it could easily throw us off. Maybe we can make some sort of harness.' He pulled off his cloak and began tearing it into thick strips. 'Tear yours up, too. We'll just have to tie ourselves onto it.'

I did so reluctantly. It was a good idea, but it really did mean we had to get home before nightfall or we would freeze to death. I was shivering already.

Once we had a knotty length of black rope I asked, 'Now what? We're still no closer to that bird.'

Rodden looked up at it again. 'We'll have to call it down. There's nothing for it. It won't be easy to pull it off its nest, though.'

'We can't do it here, there's no space for it to land.'

'Outside the tors then. We can both call it while you keep your bow trained on the entrance. The harmings can only come through single file so you can pick them off one by one.'

'And we'll just hope that once I've shot the only four arrows I have the others will trip over the dead harmings and brain themselves on the rocks?'

'Something like that.'

Our plans were getting worse.

Very carefully and quietly, I explained the plan to Griffin and Leap. I added that if anything were to happen to Rodden and me they were to get far, far away. I told them there was probably still forest on the northern side of the tors and it would be full of lovely, juicy rats. They were to stay there, and . . .

I felt the urge to cry again and I stood up quickly, praying that whatever happened, they would be safe.

'All right,' I said hoarsely. 'Let's get this over with.'

Outside the tors, Rodden broke a large stick from a tree. It sizzled in his gloved hands and he put it down quickly. 'Once you're out of arrows, use the bow to beat them off. I'll use the stick. Just keep fighting. I don't think they have weapons and they'll be weak from hunger.'

We were weak from hunger too, and fatigued. It had been a long time since we'd eaten a proper meal or had a drink of water, and last night's blood seemed a long time ago. Our plan was desperate and clumsy, but I tried to feel as confident as Rodden looked.

He tied the knotted rope firmly around my waist and left the other end lying on the ground.

'What about you?'

'It's too dangerous to tie ourselves together. I'll tie you to the brant and then just hold on to you.'

I didn't like that at all. What if the brant took off without warning and he was left on the ground? I opened my mouth to protest, but closed it again. The odds of us staying alive long enough to get on the brant were slim. I took comfort in the knowledge that the harmings would probably tear us limb from limb rather than take us captive. Being dead was infinitely preferable to being Turned.

I suddenly understood the meaning of 'fate worse than death'.

I crouched and stuck three arrows into the ground, points down, at easy grabbing distance. The fourth I notched up and aimed at the entrance, ten yards away. Rodden stood beside me. The pass curved slightly so we wouldn't see the harmings until they were most of the way along it.

He gave my shoulder a squeeze. 'Ready?'

My stomach was in turmoil. I was sure there was something critical we were forgetting, but I nodded. Together we found the brant-thread and began a summoning command. Instantly I felt the bird's reluctance. It was unsettled by the storm and its chick was fretful because of Griffin's presence in the nest all night. We kept our walls up around our minds, but the harmings were monitoring the brants just as Rodden had predicted. From inside the valley I felt a hundred minds prick up. The harmings listened for a split second, recognised us with a roar of outrage and began to swarm towards the pass. They were voracious, angry, and had murder on their minds.

I tried not to be distracted from persuading the brant and keeping aim but the harmings began beating at the wall I had put up. They were trying to break it down, force me into submission by their sheer numbers. My hold on the brant wavered as I felt the first harmings approaching the pass. The bird screamed in defiance.

There were harmings in the pass, now. Seven of them. They were running at full-tilt. My fear made me lose my grip on the brant. I cast around desperately for the thread, but then I saw the harmings and I loosed three arrows in quick succession. Three harmings fell to the ground, dead, and I was just about to fire my last arrow when I saw the others fall back out of sight.

I heard the beat of wings. The brant was airborne. I felt it approaching. Rodden was using all his concentration to guide it down to us. I kept my arrow trained on the pass.

But we had forgotten something. From behind us I heard a skittering of stones. In worrying about the harmings in the valley we had forgotten to guard our backs. I turned, saw a group of three harmings and fired. I'd panicked and my aim was off, and I merely struck one a glancing blow in the arm. The yelbar in the point was enough to make it scream in pain and fall to its knees.

That was it. I was out of arrows.

Wings beat the air. The sky overhead darkened. The other two harmings shrank back. I guessed that they were un-Turned and weren't yet used to the enormous birds.

I looked back at the pass. Four harmings were at the mouth of the pass and bearing down at us. Two skidded to a halt when the brant landed. The other two didn't falter. I heard an irate screech and Griffin attacked one with her razor-sharp beak and talons.

'Get on the brant!' Rodden yelled to me.

I clambered aboard the bird and Leap jumped up after me. The brant was skittish of the commotion and I tried to calm it with my mind. I saw Rodden reach for the stick and smash it over the head of the other harming. The branch broke instantly but the harming reeled back in pain, its face bloodied. I threw the rope to Rodden and he passed it around the brant's middle and tossed the end to me.

'Tie yourself on,' he called, and ducked away from a vicious swipe.

'Here!' I threw him my bow. He caught it and landed a few good blows. I saw the part-harmings overcome their fear of the brant and begin to approach. There was no way we could withstand an attack from all of them at once. I felt panic rise in my chest. We had to get away *now*.

'Get up here!' I yelled. Griffin alighted on my wrist and I reached the other hand to Rodden. The brant began to flap its wings. It was about to leap into the sky. Rodden grabbed my hand, kicked a harming in the face and sprang up behind me.

Go! we both shouted at the brant. It took off. At the last second a harming grabbed my leg and hung on. The weight was too much for the bird and it became stuck, three feet from the ground, its wings straining. Clawed fingers stuck in my trousers, dug into my flesh. Rodden beat the harming viciously with the bow and it let go before the others could swarm the bird. The brant's wings beat a little faster and we began to rise. The ground fell away. I watched with relief as the harmings became little more than upturned faces on the rocky ground.

I slumped over the brant's neck, overcome by exhaustion and relief. Rodden steered the brant, the tors at our backs. As the ocean came into view I held tightly to the bird's feathers, hoping that it wasn't going to dump us into the open sea. The sun was directly overhead and the water glittered like diamonds.

I felt the cord that joined me to the tors tighten and then reluctantly, agonisingly, lengthen. My breath came in painful gasps. I squeezed my eyes shut and braced against the pain. Spots danced before my eyes.

I must have blacked out for the rest of the flight because the next thing I knew I was being jolted awake by our impact with the ground. I looked around. We were in the courtyard of the palace at Xallentaria.

Leap jumped off first. Rodden slid down and worked at the knots that tied me to the brant. The rope slithered away and he helped me down. I stood on rubbery legs, my face pressed into his filthy shirt. He put his arms around me and we stood, motionless, his heart beating in my ears, until I heard Renata calling my name.

FIFTEEN

I woke several times over the next day, marvelled groggily at the soft bed and my clean hair, and then fell straight back to sleep.

Late on the second day, I struggled out from between the sheets and into the living room. Renata was there, reading a book. Everything was too sharp, too bright, too *normal*, I stared at her, remembering what Rodden had said when I'd asked how he thought I'd become a harming. *Ask your mother.* Had she known all along that I was like this and done nothing to warn me? To help me?

Renata saw me hovering in the doorway. She got up and handed me a flask. 'That man said you would need this.'

I took it. 'Do you know . . .?'

'What's in it? Yes. Go on.' She folded her arms.

'I can leave the room,' I offered.

She shook her head.

I took a few sips, feeling her eyes on me. My skin crawled with shame. I screwed the lid back on and put the flask down, my eyes averted. I couldn't do it in front of her.

'We can manage this,' Renata said, her voice brisk. 'No one need know. A special tonic in the morning is hardly unusual. The Queen of Pergamia herself has a blend of herbs she makes into a tea and drinks before breakfast every morning.' She frowned. 'Wipe your mouth, darling.'

I rubbed at my lips with the back of my hand.

'I'll have a word to the kitchen as soon as we get home –'

My heart sank.

'– and everything will be arranged. Being . . . what you are . . . is no reason you can't have a normal life.' She must have seen the shock on my face, as she added, 'It's all right, darling. Nobody else knows. Not Lilith. Well, Amis and the king know everything. They know Rodden is one of them, too. They always have.'

'How did this happen? Being sick as a baby had nothing to do with it, did it? I asked Lilith what I had and it sounded like the hundred-day cough.'

'It was the hundred-day cough that did it, but not directly.'

'What do you mean?'

Renata sighed. 'I'd just lost your father. You were barely six months old. The coughing was terrible. I was watching you die, and it was the worst time of my life. Worse than losing Garrick. I heard of a travelling apothecary who carried a magical cure with him. Any sickness or injury could be banished, just like that. So I sent for him. Your nurse warned me not to. She said she'd heard terrible things about him. People going mad and disappearing. Killing their entire families. He was very strange. Frightening, even. But I was desperate. He kept his hood up the whole time. We gave you a few drops of this dark liquid – I insisted that it be the tiniest, tiniest amount – and the effect was instantaneous.'

I was silent, picturing the scene. The harming hovering over my cradle. How could she have let such a creature near her child?

'It was a last resort, my darling. You wouldn't be here today if I hadn't done what I did.' Her blue eyes were wide, imploring. She wanted my forgiveness. She wanted me to understand.

I didn't know if I was ready for that. 'You know what that man was? A harming.'

'I couldn't let you die, Zeraphina. And look at you – you're fine. Nothing needs to change.'

I stood up and went to the window, my fists clenched at my sides. Fine? I was fine? I didn't *feel* fine. I could sense them now, the tors, tugging at my insides. I remembered the Lharmellins' haunting song. 'Why didn't you tell me what I was?' My voice shook.

'Darling, I didn't know.'

'You're lying. The books in the library. You said you knew none of them contained a mention of Lharmell. How could you know that if you didn't personally see to it?'

'No one is allowed books on that place. It is forbidden.' She came up behind me and placed her hands on my shoulders. 'I would never lie to you. Darling, you must believe me.'

She would have tried to help me if she thought there was anything wrong. Wouldn't she?

'You never showed any sign that I should have worried about you. Your hair and eyes – they seemed little more than an inconvenient side effect. And it happened such a long time ago. Can't we just forget about it?'

'I can't forget! It's inside me. It's changed me.' But she was right about something: I had been far,

far too good at hiding what I really was. No wonder she didn't understand.

'Yesterday I arranged for our things to be packed up,' she said. 'We're leaving for Amentia tomorrow.'

Fear clawed at my chest. The tor-line wrenched painfully. I had expected a barrage of questions, for her to demand to hear everything that had happened to me since the night of the ball. She didn't want to know. She wanted things to proceed exactly as if nothing unpleasant had ever happened, just as she always did. I needed nothing more than a tonic in the mornings and I could go home with her and be a dutiful daughter. Marry someone who I would have to deceive for the rest of my life. How could I forget everything I'd seen? How could I do nothing now that I knew the truth?

'Mother, I don't think I can go home.'

'Is it because of that man?' Her voice was sharp. 'Did anything happen between the two of you that I should know about?'

I rounded on her. 'You should be thanking "that man" for my life. He was the one who came to find me in Lharmell. I wouldn't be alive if it wasn't for him.' Outwardly I bristled; inwardly, the truth squirmed in my belly. I realised I didn't just feel gratitude towards Rodden. I felt affinity. He was like me. He could understand what I had been through. The thought of suffering the pain of returning to Amentia was bad enough – but to be there alone? It was too much.

'I can't go home right now. I don't think I can ever go home.'

I heard footsteps running in the hall outside, and then the door was flung open.

'Fina!' Lilith wrapped both her arms around me.

Over her shoulder, Renata was watching us with a look of resignation in her eyes.

'Lilith,' I said tentatively, 'what would you think if I didn't go home with Mother just yet. If I stayed on and –'

Lilith pulled back, looking at me in surprise.

'Only if you want the company that is,' I said.

She flung her arms around me again. 'Yes! Yes, I do. I was so worried what I should do in a big castle full of so many strangers, but having you here would make all the difference. Isn't it wonderful, Mother?'

Renata gave a tight smile and turned away. Lilith, oblivious, kept right on hugging me.

———

I found him on the northern parapet. The sun was setting in the west and there was a fresh wind blowing off the sea. It was a natural wind, the only sounds carried on it were the rustling of leaves and the evening chorus of birds. I heard the plaintive cry of a peacock from the gardens.

Rodden was leaning on the battlements, watching the northern horizon. Dark shapes were in the sky.

I stood beside him. 'What's happening?'

'It's the brants,' he said. 'The Lharmellin's have lost their grip on them. They're flying away, for now.'

'For now?'

He nodded. 'They'll go back. Lharmell is their home.'

'Did we do that?'

He smiled. 'We sure did.'

'Renata told me what happened when I was a baby.'

'You were dying and some nice hooded figure offered her a miracle cure?'

I nodded.

'Thought so.'

I looked towards the tors. 'Do you think it will ever stop?'

He knew what I meant: the blood-hunger, the bond with Lharmell, the innocent people killed or turned into harmings. He was silent for a moment, his ice-blue eyes bleak. 'Perhaps. It's too soon to know if what we did will have any effect.'

I nodded, and slipped the ring off my thumb, the one he'd stolen all those weeks ago. I held it out to him.

He took it, frowning. 'What's this, something to remember you by?'

I shook my head. 'I'm not going anywhere. This is my fight, too. I just want to make sure that if something happens, you'll have a way of finding me. And me you.' I waited for him to argue with me. To tell me to go home. Forget everything.

I'd had enough of people trying to make me forget who I was. But I could no more forget the ground beneath my feet.

He looked at the small silver band, turning it this way and that. Then he smiled. 'I think I've got a pretty good fix on you already, Zeraphina.' He slipped the ring onto his finger. 'But I'll hang on to it, just in case.'

I watched the dark shapes of the brants circling on the horizon. They wouldn't stray far from Lharmell. They just weren't able.

ACKNOWLEDGEMENTS

Thanks must go to the following people who helped make this book what it is today, and kept me sane.

All the staff and students of RMIT's Professional Writing and Editing course, particularly Clare Renner and the students of the 2009 Writing For Young Adults class.

The blogosphere and Twitterverse, without whom this journey would have been a lot lonelier.

The authors Amanda Ashby and R. A. Nelson for holding my hand across the miles.

The Random House Australia team for their enthusiasm, particularly Zoe Walton, my publisher, for taking a chance on a first-time author, and Abigail Nathan and Kimberley Bennett for their keen editorial eyes and helping me see the bigger picture.

My agent Ginger Clark. It seems obvious to say I couldn't have done this without her, but I really couldn't have done this without her.

The early readers of the manuscript who got me excited about the project and gave invaluable insights, including Shona Cameron, Megan Davis, Benjamin Harlow, Robert Hart, Michael Kimpton, Robert Lawlor, Reannon Shaw, Libby Stewart, Sandi Worrall-Hart and Melissa Wren.

The later readers, who kept my hopes alive, and are too numerous to list.

My dear friends for keeping me sane and, best of all, for being proud of me.

All my family, but particularly my mum and dad, for teaching me to read, reading to me, for a childhood surrounded by books, and for making me who I am today.

ABOUT THE AUTHOR

Rhiannon Hart remembers writing before she could read, puzzling over the strange squiggles in *Jeremiah and the Dark Woods* by Janet and Alan Ahlberg and putting her own words in their places. Her first love was Jareth the Goblin King at the tender age of eight. She wrote fan fiction in high school but she'd never admit to it out loud, so don't ask. When she's not reading or writing she is belly dancing, chasing after other people's cats, or putting the pedal to the floor at her sewing machine. She grew up in north-western Australia and currently resides in Melbourne, where she works in marketing. Rhiannon has been published in the *Australian Book Review*, *Magpies* and *Viewpoint* and blogs at http://rhiannon-hart.blogspot.com/.